Jadon glanced at that moment the intimacy, a bon to the soles of his feet.

Together they'd created these baby girls.

Looking at Alyssa holding Grace, and the way Gretchen slept so peacefully in his arms, he realized what he'd told her earlier was true. There was no turning back. He was a father now.

This new, precious family was a part of his future. His and Alyssa's future.

If only he knew how in the world he was going to make it work…

Dear Reader

Welcome to **Cedar Bluff Hospital**, located in a small Wisconsin town overlooking the beautiful rocky shores of Lake Michigan. EXPECTING A CHRISTMAS MIRACLE is the second book in my new mini-series. I really hope you enjoy reading about Alyssa and Jadon as much as I enjoyed writing about them.

Alyssa and Jadon had a hot, brief affair that ended when Jadon left without a word. When Alyssa discovered she was pregnant with twins, she tried to reach Jadon—but couldn't. Resigned to raising her babies alone, she is shocked and surprised when Jadon unexpectedly returns to his job as one of the emergency department doctors on staff. Alyssa is determined to remain independent, but she soon realises she needs Jadon's help. When the babies arrive prematurely, Alyssa and Jadon are drawn together as they fight for their tiny babies to survive. Somehow they must find a way to heal the wounds of the past in order to save their new family.

I hope you enjoy EXPECTING A CHRISTMAS MIRACLE, and look for the third book in my **Cedar Bluff Hospital** series, to come next month with a New Year's story.

Happy Reading!

Laura

EXPECTING
A CHRISTMAS
MIRACLE

BY
LAURA IDING

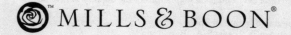

MILLS & BOON®

First published in Great Britain 2009
Harlequin Mills & Boon Limited,
Eton House, 18-24 Paradise Road, Richmond, Surrey TW9 1SR

© Laura Iding 2009

ISBN: 978 0 263 86880 7

Set in Times Roman 10½ on 12¾ pt
03-1109-44807

Harlequin Mills & Boon policy is to use papers that are natural, renewable and recyclable products and made from wood grown in sustainable forests. The logging and manufacturing process conform to the legal environmental regulations of the country of origin.

Printed and bound in Spain
by Litografia Rosés, S.A., Barcelona

Laura Iding loved reading as a child, and when she ran out of books she readily made up her own, completing a little detective mini-series when she was twelve. But, despite her aspirations for being an author, her parents insisted she look into a 'real' career. So the summer after she turned thirteen she volunteered as a Candy Striper, and fell in love with nursing. Now, after twenty years of experience in trauma/critical care, she's thrilled to combine her career and her hobby into one—writing Medical™ Romances for Mills & Boon. Laura lives in the northern part of the United States, and spends all her spare time with her two teenage kids (help!)—a daughter and a son—and her husband.

Recent titles by the same author:

MARRYING THE PLAYBOY DOCTOR*
EMERGENCY: SINGLE DAD, MOTHER NEEDED
THE SURGEON'S SECRET BABY WISH
THE FIREFIGHTER AND THE SINGLE MUM

*Cedar Bluff Hospital

This book is dedicated to my editor Meg Lewis.
Thanks for everything.
I always enjoy working with you.

CHAPTER ONE

"SLOW down, Ben," Alyssa Knight called, tightening the red wool scarf around her neck and pulling her black jacket over her pregnant belly in an effort to block the chilly wind as she followed her charge down the path toward the Lake Michigan shoreline. "I can't move that fast."

"But I want to see if the water is frozen," Ben protested, with six-year-old logic.

"The lake is too large to freeze. Ben, I mean it. Stop right there and wait for me," Alyssa said in a firm, you'd-better-listen tone.

Ben let out a heavy sigh and stopped in the middle of the path. She smiled and shook her head. Ben was Kylie Germaine's active son, and she'd agreed to watch him for a few hours. Kylie was spending this Saturday afternoon doing some last-minute Christmas shopping, along with a final fitting for her wedding dress, in preparation for her New Year's Eve wedding to Seth Taylor, one of Cedar Bluff's Emergency Department physicians.

Kylie would make a beautiful bride, she thought with a pang of envy. The couple radiated happiness. When

Alyssa had been young, she'd always wished for a big family. Kylie and Seth were planning to have more kids, and Seth already treated Ben like his own son.

She was glad to help out, even for a couple of hours.

There was an inch of snow covering the ground and she was looking forward to a white Christmas. In spite of the chill in the cold December air, she'd thought a trip to Cedar Bluff Park would be a good way to keep Ben occupied. Much better than sitting around in her small apartment.

An apartment too small for her expanding family.

The dark, heavy clouds overhead indicated more snow might be on the way. She picked up her pace, more so to keep warm than to catch up with Ben.

"When are your babies going to be born?" Ben asked as she met up with him on the path. There was an upper path leading to the top of the bluff overlooking Lake Michigan, but they'd taken the lower path leading directly to the lakeshore. Climbing the upper path in her current condition had been too daunting.

"Not for another eight weeks," she told him, smoothing her hand down over her stomach. At least she hoped she wouldn't have them too early. With twins, nothing was certain. Not only was she facing the fact she was pregnant with twins, but that she'd need to raise them alone, since their father, an emergency department physician named Jadon Reichert, had vanished in a disappearing act over four months ago.

She'd tried to call him, to let him know she was pregnant, but after the first couple of messages his cell phone had announced the number was out of service. According to Seth, Jadon was on an extended personal leave of absence from Cedar Bluff Hospital. In her opinion, a personal leave of absence was nothing more than a euphemism for gone and never coming back.

Which meant she was on her own. Exactly how she would manage to raise two kids alone was something she hadn't quite figured out yet. But, no matter what, she was determined to succeed in providing her babies with a secure, loving home.

"Mom says you're gonna need our help when the babies are born," Ben said, skipping up the path. He picked up a large stick and poked it into the snow.

She was going to need help all right. And lots of it. Luckily the close-knit, family-like atmosphere of Cedar Bluff, the town and the hospital where she worked as an ED/trauma nurse, meant she was surrounded by friends. People like Kylie and Seth had already offered their support.

Alyssa knew she wasn't alone. Not really. But having friends who were willing to chip in and help wasn't exactly the same as having a full-time father for her babies.

Wishing for the impossible was a waste of time, so she quickly pushed thoughts of Jadon aside. She'd gone into the affair knowing it wasn't going to last, so it was her own fault if her heart had gotten bruised when he'd left. If he didn't want to be a part of her life, fine. Her focus needed to be on taking care of herself and the babies.

Besides, her favorite holiday of all, Christmas, was only a few weeks away.

The path opened into a small clearing near the lakefront. Ben dashed forward, heading straight for the rocky shore.

"Don't go near the water," she warned.

"I won't," he hollered over his shoulder.

She told herself not to worry so much. Kylie brought Ben down to the lakefront all the time; surely he would abide by his mother's limitations. The wind kicked up, blasting frigid air into her face, whipping her long dark hair over her eyes and stealing her breath.

Jiminy Cricket, it was cold.

She turned to face the wind, pushing her hair out of her eyes. She pulled the scarf around her neck a little tighter and looked for Ben. Where had he gone? Impatiently she scanned the area, finding him standing precariously on the rocks above the water.

What part of *Don't go near the water* hadn't he understood?

"Ben? What are you doing?" she called in exasperation. "Get down and come back here."

He didn't seem to hear her, poking intently at something between the rocks. She had no idea what he'd found—surely all the marine wildlife was in hibernation by early December. She quickened her step, intent on dragging him back to safety, when suddenly there was a loud crack and a shrill cry. His walking stick had snapped in two, throwing him off balance. His small arms made windmill motions as he hung for mind-numbing seconds poised above the water.

"Ben!" Alyssa broke into a run just as his body toppled into the icy lake with a horrifying splash.

She scrambled up and over the rocks, helplessly scanning the water for his body. Could he swim? Had he hit a rock? Could he survive in the dangerously cold water?

There, his tiny head bobbed in the water, his arms flailing as he tried to stay afloat, his heavy winter coat dragging him down. Quickly, she shrugged out of her coat and pulled off her scarf. Remembering some of her old lifeguard skills, she wound one end of the scarf around her left hand and leaned out as far as she dared before tossing the other end into the water toward Ben.

"Grab the scarf!" she shouted. "I'll pull you in."

Ben reached for the end of the scarf, but missed. Her heart lodged in her throat when his head disappeared beneath the water for a couple of long seconds. Thankfully, the tide pushed him a little closer as his head cleared the surface again.

"Ben!" She reeled in the scarf and this time took careful aim before throwing it again, hitting him in the chest. "Grab the scarf!"

In slow motion, his numb fingers grasped the end and she nearly wept with relief as she towed him the short distance to shore. "I've got you. It's all right, I've got you."

When he was close enough to the edge, she reached down to pull him up.

Her center of gravity shifted. She'd forgotten all about her pregnant belly and her miscalculation made her lose her balance. She plopped with a thud into the water next to Ben.

Her babies!

Shockingly cold water surrounded her, sucking her down into the murky depths. For precious seconds she couldn't move, stunned by the cold water, and she idly wondered if she and Ben were both going to drown. The thought spurred her into action. Frantically she strove toward the surface, her fingertips brushing against something soft. Ben. Her head cleared the surface and she coughed, grabbing hold of the boy and holding him upright in the water.

"I've got you," she repeated, gasping and clenching her jaw to keep her teeth from chattering. Poor Ben had already been in the frigid water too long for a child his size. She tried not to think about the potential harm to her unborn children as she shucked off Ben's water-soaked coat so he'd weigh less and then used every ounce of her strength to lever him upright, literally pushing him up and out of the lake, onto the rocks. "See my coat up there? Use it to get warm."

Ben crawled over the rocks, falling facedown onto her coat. He may have been out of the water, but he still wasn't safe. Hypothermia was deadly. He needed to get warm, and soon.

Alyssa struggled to follow him out and over the rocks, but her fingers slipped and she fell back into the water, her strength seeping away. Desperately, she lunged upward, clutching a boulder while also trying to find a toehold so she could climb out. The task seemed impossible. She didn't have the upper-arm strength to pull herself out of the water.

Her legs were numb. She focused on Ben's too-still body lying on her coat and on the survival of her babies to give her the energy and willpower she needed to pull herself out of the icy water. She had to do this. She had to! She found a toehold and inched her way up, willing the quivering muscles in her arms to support her.

Finally she broke free of the icy prison, dragging herself up, over the rocks to safety.

"Ben." She collapsed next to him, beyond shivering

as the cold wind hit her wet body. She recognized the numbing fatigue for the danger it presented. They needed help. Fast.

Her fingers didn't move very well, but she managed to pry her cell phone out of her coat pocket and fumbled to flip it open. Pushing the buttons for 911 wasn't easy, but she had to try. She couldn't rest, not until she'd told someone where they were.

Dimly she realized the connection had been made. The dispatcher wanted to know the nature of her emergency. "We're on the rocks by the lakeshore in Cedar Bluff Park. We fell in the water. Hypothermia. Hurry…"

The woman dispatcher on the other end of the line continued talking, but Alyssa couldn't hang on to the phone, uncaring when it clattered against the rocks, disappearing from view. Help was on the way, all they had to do was wait. She pulled Ben against her rounded stomach, sharing what little warmth they possessed between them and doing her best to use her coat to shelter his body from the dangerously cold wind.

"Don't worry, they're coming to get us," she whispered, closing her eyes, the need to sleep nearly overwhelming. "They're coming…"

Bright lights. Blurred faces. Unintelligible voices.

Warmth. Lifesaving warmth.

Exhaustion. Her arms and legs felt like dead weights. Even her head was too heavy. Tired. She was so very, very tired.

Time had no meaning. She vaguely realized she was probably at the hospital. Maybe still in the emergency department. The people around her were a blur. She needed to know if Ben was all right, but couldn't find the strength to ask.

"Alyssa? Can you hear me?"

She frowned, blinking against the light, recognizing a familiar face hovering above her.

Jadon?

No, it must be her mind playing tricks on her. Jadon was gone. He'd left.

He was on a personal leave of absence. Gone for months. And never coming back. He didn't know she was pregnant. He didn't know he was soon to be the father of twins.

"Alyssa? Look at me. Can you hear me?"

No, she didn't want to do this. She didn't want to keep having dreams about Jadon. They were too painful. She closed her eyes and turned away, seeking peace.

Allowing the precious warmth to draw her down into blessed oblivion.

Jadon Reichert clutched Alyssa's limp hand in his and willed her to open her eyes, to talk to him.

"We need to get her moved up to the OB unit," Kim Rayborn was saying. She was the OB doctor on call, responding to emergencies as needed, but had informed him that she was also Alyssa's regular OB doctor.

Pregnant.

Alyssa was pregnant.

With twins. His twins.

The irony of the situation didn't escape him. He was certain, without talking to Alyssa, that the babies were his. The timing was right, for one thing. He'd thought they'd been careful, but obviously not careful enough. How could this have happened? With everything else in his life falling apart, he hadn't even considered the possibility he'd left her pregnant.

Even now, when faced with the reality of Alyssa's round belly, his mind couldn't seem to grasp the news. He'd told Alyssa from the start he wasn't looking for a long-term relationship, and she'd agreed that she wasn't either. But things had quickly gotten intense between them. When he'd received the emergency call from his mother, he'd left Cedar Bluff, figuring the timing was for the best, since he'd been starting to care about Alyssa a little too much.

Now he was back. And Alyssa was pregnant. She and Ben had been rushed into the ED by the paramedics, both requiring immediate treatment for hypothermia on the same day he was being reoriented to the ED by Simon Carter, one of the other ED physicians.

He'd soon learned that Ben was Kylie and Seth's son. Kylie was relatively new to Cedar Bluff so he'd never met her, but he'd worked with Seth Taylor. The boy had been dangerously chilled after his dunking in the icy lake water, but he'd be all right. Seth had been home sleeping after his night shift, but he'd rushed in to be there for Ben, with Kylie showing up a little while later.

The boy would be fine. And so would Alyssa.

Kim Rayborn hadn't made a similar commitment regarding the survival of Alyssa's twins yet.

As much as he'd never considered being a father, he was oddly protective of his unborn babies now.

"We need to move her upstairs to the OB unit," Kim repeated, as if he were a dimwitted child.

"I know," he said, in a hoarse voice. "But I'd like to stay with her."

Kim's expression held uncertainty. "Jadon, Alyssa has been through a terrible shock. Maybe it's best for now to give her some time, some space. Why don't you let her get through this immediate crisis first?" Before disrupting her life, was her unspoken implication.

She was right. Logically, he knew Kim was right. Yet he didn't want to let go of Alyssa's hand, to let her be taken upstairs without him. The OB specialist had already confirmed his fear regarding the possibility of premature labor. Alyssa had nearly lost her life. Right now, she needed to conserve her strength.

Clearly, she wasn't ready to talk to him.

Alyssa had looked directly into his eyes when he'd called her name. The way she'd turned from him, deliberately closing her eyes to shut him out, had stabbed deep. But at the same time he understood she had every right to be angry.

Heaven help him, he hadn't known she was pregnant when he'd left.

And what in the heck were they going to do about it now that he knew? He couldn't even imagine how they'd move forward from here.

"All right," he said, prising his fingers from Alyssa's and taking a step back. "But please keep me updated on her progress."

Kim nodded. "As much as I can. You already know she's starting to have mild contractions. We're going to see if we can stop them from getting any worse. But I have to be honest, once she's awake, it will be up to her to decide how much information you'll receive."

He clenched his teeth, wanting to protest, but held his tongue. The health-care privacy laws had been in place for several years. As a physician he knew them well, had explained them to many a distraught family member.

But he'd never been on the receiving end of their restrictions until now. He tamped down the helpless anger at how government rules could keep him away from Alyssa and their unborn babies.

Kim snapped orders and the nurses scurried to prepare Alyssa to be transported up to the OB unit. Standing in the middle of the ED and watching her go was difficult.

"Are you all right?" Simon asked, clapping a hand on his shoulder.

"Sure," he lied, glancing around the ED. Now that Alyssa and Ben had been cared for, the activity level had returned to normal. Almost as if nothing had ever happened. The staff were already getting things cleaned up in preparation for the next emergency. "Is there anything else we need to review?"

Simon's gaze rose questioningly, not entirely believing he was fine, as he shook his head. "No, I think you've got it covered. You're cleared to be placed on the physician schedule."

"Great." Jadon was relieved. Work was what he'd wanted, what he'd craved during the months he'd been gone. He'd known he'd have to work with Alyssa again, and that probably things would be awkward between them after the way he'd left abruptly. But her pregnancy changed everything. He couldn't pretend their passion had burned itself out and he'd decided to move on without her. "Thanks."

"Maybe you should head home for a while," Simon suggested. "I'm sure you have plenty of other things to get caught up with since you've been gone."

He did, but nothing as important as Alyssa and her unborn children, fighting for their lives upstairs in the OB unit. For a man who hadn't wanted a family, he couldn't seem to get Alyssa and her babies out of his mind.

"Nah, I think I'll hang around here for a while." He couldn't make himself leave. Not yet. "Maybe I'll grab something to eat in the cafeteria." He didn't have anything to eat in his house anyway. The place had been closed up for months.

Simon nodded. "See you later, then."

Jadon wandered down to the cafeteria, not really hungry but desperate for something to do. He stared at the various meal selections before finally deciding upon a bowl of steaming hot chili. He'd barely sat down with his meal when he heard his name over the loudspeaker.

"Jadon Reichert, please report to the OB unit. Jadon Reichert, please report to the OB unit immediately."

Alyssa!

He jumped up, abandoning his food, and headed for the stairs. He ran all the way up to the fifth floor, his heart pounding from exertion as much as fear.

"I'm Jadon Reichert. You paged me? About a patient, Alyssa Knight?" he said to the clerk seated at the front desk.

"Yes, Dr. Rayborn was looking for you." The clerk picked up the phone and dialed. "Dr. Rayborn? Jadon Reichert is here."

Within moments Kim appeared, dressed in scrubs

and an ultra-serious expression. He clenched his hands into fists and braced himself for the news.

"I've started Alyssa on a continuous infusion of ter-butaline in an attempt to stop her contractions," Kim explained. "They're getting less severe, but haven't stopped yet. If I'm not successful in halting her labor over the next twenty-four hours, you need to know there is a good chance Alyssa will end up delivering her twins prematurely."

CHAPTER TWO

WAITING was pure, interminable hell.

Jadon paced the small waiting room located near the delivery suites. Kim had insisted on keeping Alyssa in the labor and delivery area until she was certain she could stop Alyssa's labor. Especially since Alyssa hadn't fully recovered from her hypothermic episode.

Not knowing what was going on behind the closed doors was killing him. He was a man who liked to be in control. He didn't know how to be patient. After he'd practically worn a path in the carpeting, he finally sat, dropping his head into his hands with a low groan.

There was no reason to dwell constantly on the potential complications. Alyssa would be fine. And even if the babies came early, they weren't too small. Kim had estimated one twin to be about three pounds, the other about three and a half pounds.

About the same size he and Jack had been.

He closed his eyes on a wave of despair. He didn't want to think about his twin brother, or about Jack's problems.

Especially since he hadn't been entirely truthful with Alyssa. She knew he had a brother, but she didn't know Jack was his identical twin.

The lie of omission had stuck in his throat, even back then. But he'd gotten so used to hiding the truth over the years, especially where women were concerned. The stress of coping with his brother had destroyed too many relationships. The breakup of his own brief engagement was bad enough, but the failure of his parents' marriage had driven the lesson home. Relationships didn't work for someone in his situation and covering up the truth made it easier to avoid lengthy explanations.

No matter how much he wished otherwise, his life wasn't his own. Jack would always have to come first. It wouldn't be right to bring anyone else into his messed-up family.

But then he'd met Alyssa. He'd told himself to stay away, but he hadn't seemed to be able to resist her. He had broken their rule of no strings by falling for her.

And now Alyssa was pregnant with his babies.

With twins.

Worry gnawed a hole in the lining of his stomach. If he could go back and do things differently, he would. He wouldn't have left so abruptly, responding instantly to his mother's panicked phone call the way he always had before. He would have talked to Alyssa first, taken the time to formally break things off between them.

But he still would have left Cedar Bluff.

Jack had needed him. There'd been no choice but to leave.

"Jadon?"

Hearing his name, he glanced up and rose to his feet. Kim's gaze was warm, and relief flowed over him as he sensed good news. "Yes?"

"Alyssa's labor seems to have slowed down significantly and her membranes are still intact. I'm fairly confident we won't have to deliver the babies for a while yet, although we're going to continue to watch her closely overnight, just in case."

Thank God. Relief was overwhelming. "Alyssa's awake? She's feeling fine?"

"Well, she's still pretty sleepy. I don't know that she's fully recovered from her ordeal."

"I'd like to see her," he said firmly.

Kim hesitated. "Jadon, Alyssa confided in me that you were the father of her babies, which is why I've kept you in the loop about her condition. But now, since it seems she's stabilized, I think it's best if we hold off on any confrontations until she's stronger."

Confrontations? "Give me a little credit, Kim. I'm not going to argue with her. I just want to know how she's doing." And let her know he was sorry he'd left without saying goodbye.

"Wait until tomorrow," Kim advised. "Alyssa's been through enough of a shock for the moment. It's better if you give her a little time to rest."

Leaving Alyssa without seeing her went against every instinct he possessed. Yet clearly Kim felt she was acting in her patient's best interests. Knowing further arguments weren't going to get him anywhere, he let out a deep sigh and nodded.

"All right, I'll wait. But if she does wake up, please let her know I'm anxious to see her."

Kim pursed her lips thoughtfully. "And if she doesn't want to see you?" she asked.

Panic gripped him by the throat. Obviously he

couldn't force Alyssa to see him. To talk to him. To let him explain. And even if she did, what could he offer her? Nothing but heartache. Yet he had to help take care of his babies. "She will." He forced a confidence he was far from feeling.

"All right, Jadon. We'll see what tomorrow brings."

He could tell Alyssa's OB doctor wasn't convinced. Heck, neither was he. All he could do was hope Alyssa would give him a few minutes of her time to explain, as best he could, without going into too much detail.

He didn't want to add to her stress by disclosing the entire truth. She had enough to worry about at the moment.

He couldn't believe she would ignore him completely, not when they both knew he was the babies' father. They hadn't wanted a future, but here they were anyway. Somehow they needed to find a way to get along, at least enough to provide a secure, loving environment for their children.

Feeling grim, he was forced to acknowledge it was a task much easier said than done.

Alyssa awoke feeling groggy and disoriented, as if she'd slept for days instead of mere hours. What time was it anyway?

She scanned the room, looking for a clock, but quickly realized she wasn't in the ED. The bright yellow walls and the warm decor, including the snowflakes and "Merry Christmas" written on the windows in white spray-on snow, didn't look at all familiar. She lifted her head, trying to find a nurse, instinctively placing a hand over her swollen abdomen.

She smoothed a hand over her stomach, searching for the familiar movements from deep within her womb. After a few moments relief washed over her as she felt the babies moving. She and the babies had managed to survive their swim in Lake Michigan.

And Ben, too?

Panic made her suck in a harsh breath. What about Ben? What had happened to Ben?

"Is someone there?" she called out, searching in her bed for her call-light. No wonder patients felt so helpless when they didn't have their call-lights within reach.

"Yes, I'm here." A pretty nurse entered the room and Alyssa recognized her as Marla, one of the labor and delivery nurses whose husband was also one of the anesthesiologists on staff. "Don't worry, you're doing well. And your babies are doing fine, too. We've been monitoring them through fetal heart tones."

Good news about her babies. "But what about Ben?" Alyssa couldn't relax, not until she knew what had happened.

"Ben?" Marla looked perplexed for a moment, and then her expression cleared. "Oh, yes, Kylie and Seth's son, Ben. He's doing fine. I believe they kept him overnight for observation as well on the pediatric unit."

She relaxed against the pillows. "I'm so glad."

"Alyssa, it's good to see you're finally awake." Dr. Rayborn came into the room, standing beside Marla. "And of course you've been asking about Ben."

"I don't remember much once I called 911," Alyssa admitted. "I must have been out of it for a while."

Kim raised a brow. "You were. In fact, you've been sleeping all night. But don't worry, Ben woke up much quicker than you did, and he's been telling everyone who'll listen how you saved his life."

She flashed a tired smile, very glad to hear Ben was okay. She hoped Kylie would forgive her for putting Ben's life in danger in the first place. It was her fault he'd needed saving.

Now that she knew her babies and Ben were safe, she relaxed against the pillows. Through her open door she could hear the lyrical sound of hospital carolers singing "Joy to the World", one of her favorite Christmas songs. Just hearing the uplifting music made her smile.

"Alyssa." Kim's expression changed to one of concern as she reached for her hand. "There's something I need to tell you."

Her muscles suddenly tensed and her smile faded. "What?"

"Jadon's here."

"Jadon is here? In Cedar Bluff?" She stared, confused. She vaguely remembered dreaming about Jadon. Was it possible the image of his concerned face hovering over hers hadn't been a dream?

"Yes. And he wants to see you," Dr. Rayborn said. "He's back from his leave of absence, and was actually doing an orientation shift in the ED when the paramedic crew rushed you and Ben in."

Jadon was back. She hadn't been dreaming his face near hers after all. She could hardly comprehend the news. Why had he returned? And why hadn't he called, especially after she'd left him a message? Why hadn't he at least bothered to let her know he was planning to come back?

Useless questions, as only Jadon could provide the answers.

She glanced at Kim. "I assume he knows about the babies?"

Kim nodded. "You told me he was the father. Is that true?"

She momentarily closed her eyes, wishing things had been different. For her and for Jadon. Resigned, she nodded. "Yes, it's true."

"He was extremely upset when you were brought in," Kim said gently. "He was literally glued to your side during the rewarming process as we struggled to get your core temperatures up to normal. He was also very shocked to learn you were pregnant."

"Yeah, well, all he had to do was answer my messages and he would have known about my pregnancy a lot sooner." She couldn't hide the note of bitterness that crept into her tone.

"I know you're upset, but it might be good to at least hear his side of the story," Kim pointed out.

His side of the story? There was a part of her that didn't really want to know. She and Jadon hadn't spoken much about their pasts. The last thing she wanted to hear was about some wife, or ex-wife, or ex-girlfriend. While he'd been gone it had been all too easy to think the worst. And it was very hard to believe Jadon had been glued to her side in the ED, especially when he'd left four and a half months ago without a word.

No, she couldn't do it. She wasn't ready to face him. Wasn't sure she'd ever be ready.

Besides, what difference would it make to talk to him? She and Jadon didn't have a future. Things had changed during the time he'd been gone. She'd grown accustomed to being without him. Had already planned on raising her babies alone. She didn't need a man to be happy; she was more than content to focus her life on her children.

She wasn't the same person who'd loved recklessly and lost so painfully. She'd gone into an intimate relationship with Jadon, thinking she could keep things light and fun. He was handsome and charismatic, reminding her very much of her father. And he'd told her up front that he wasn't interested in anything long term either. Another factor that had reminded her of her father.

Which was exactly why she'd suspected Jadon wasn't ever coming back.

So why was he here now? Maybe he needed to see her first, before he walked away one last time. Surely discovering the news about the twins would scare him away. Did he know they were his? Or would she have to convince him through blood tests? If so, she wouldn't bother. If he didn't want to acknowledge them as his, it was fine with her.

"I'll see him later," she said, avoiding the inevitable but unable to help herself. "Are you going to discharge me soon?"

Kim hesitated and slowly shook her head. "I can't discharge you yet, Alyssa. I've had you on a continuous infusion of low-dose terbutaline to help stop your premature contractions. Once I wean you off the medication, we'll see how you do. I may be able to discharge you within the next twenty-four hours, but I'd like you to stay on bed rest for a few days."

Bed rest? Alyssa tried to hide her dismay. "I understand you're trying to prevent premature labor, but I can't work if I'm on bed rest."

"I know." Kim's warm gaze focused on hers. "I realize you need to support yourself, but the health of your unborn babies must be the highest priority."

Of course it was. Chagrined, she nodded. "You're right. I'm sorry. I'll stay on bed rest as long as you tell me I need to."

"Well, let's plan on a couple of days at least," Kim clarified. "Then we'll see how it goes. You are fairly far along in your pregnancy, but every week you carry the babies, the better their chances of survival without complications."

Alyssa knew her doctor was right. She'd make ends meet, somehow. "Okay, so when are you going to start weaning me off the medication?" she asked.

"Right now," Kim said with a smile. "Marla? Start lowering the drip rate, a few milliliters per hour, while monitoring for contractions."

"Okay." Marla made her way to make the first adjustments on the IV pump.

"Dr. Rayborn?" Alyssa called when Kim moved as if to leave.

"Yes?" She turned back toward Alyssa.

"If Jadon shows up this morning, I'll see him."

Kim raised a brow. "Are you sure? I don't blame you for needing some time."

There wasn't enough time left in all creation for her to be ready to face Jadon, and that was the God's honest truth. So she'd be better off facing him now, since she fully expected he wouldn't be sticking around much longer. He was reminding her more and more of her father, who certainly hadn't stuck around for very long. Some men just weren't meant for long-term relationships.

Once he understood she wouldn't force him into playing the role of loving father to her unborn twins, she suspected he'd do his all-too-familiar disappearing act once again.

"I'm sure."

"Jadon?"

At the sound of his name, he glanced up to find Kim standing in the entryway of the waiting room. He flashed a crooked smile. "Hi."

She raised a brow and shook her head, raking a gaze over his rumpled clothes. "Don't tell me you slept here all night?"

"Okay, I won't tell you." He stood and stretched, trying to work the kinks out of his back. "What's up?"

"Alyssa is being weaned off the terbutaline, and so far the contractions haven't returned. She'll be in the labor and delivery area for a while yet, but she's ready to see you."

She was? Alyssa was willing to see him?

He'd waited so long he'd assumed she'd decided against it.

"She knows I'm here?" he asked, suddenly extremely nervous about seeing her.

Kim nodded. "Yes, although I didn't tell her you slept here all night. But she did confirm you're the father of her babies, although if you need a formal paternity test, that can certainly be arranged."

"No. No tests. Unless Alyssa wants one." He almost blurted out the truth, about how now that he thought about it, he knew exactly when they'd conceived. The one time he and Alyssa had gotten carried away and hadn't used protection.

But this wasn't the time, or the place, or the appropriate person with which to have this conversation. He needed to talk to Alyssa first.

No matter how difficult.

"She's in Labor and Delivery room number five." Kim smiled again. "Take your time. I have patients to see in clinic this morning so I won't be back until later this afternoon, unless something changes."

He nodded, feeling nervous. He made his way back down the hall of the labor and delivery suites. The door to Alyssa's room was closed. He knocked, and then, when he couldn't hear anything, opened the door. "Alyssa? May I come in?"

"Yes." Her voice was weak, and he hesitated, wondering if his timing was bad. Maybe he should wait until she was fully recovered from her hypothermia episode.

Don't be a coward, he told himself, pushing the door open and entering her room.

Her face was pale, framed by a cloud of her dark, curly hair spread out over the pillow. She looked better than she had when the paramedic unit had brought her icy-cold, limp body through the trauma room doors.

He'd never been so scared.

"How are you feeling?" he asked, tentatively coming closer.

She lifted a shoulder and smoothed a hand over her

belly, as he'd often seen pregnant women do. There was something innately caring in her gesture. "Fine. They're telling me the babies are doing well, which is all I care about."

He didn't necessarily agree, since her well-being was very important to him, but nodded anyway. She was so beautiful, especially now, with her body soft and round with child. His gaze dropped to her lush breasts, not entirely hidden by the shapeless hospital gown she wore. They were fuller than he remembered.

He swallowed hard and dragged his glance away. What was wrong with him? Alyssa wouldn't appreciate his lustful thoughts. Especially after the way he'd left her so abruptly.

"Look, Jadon, I know you weren't expecting this." Alyssa, always direct, cut right to the heart of the matter. "But you need to know, I tried to call you. I left a message, but then the next time I called, your phone was disconnected."

"I'm sorry," he apologized, knowing she had every right to be upset as he pulled out his new cell phone. "My old cell phone was stolen." And he wasn't about to share the details of that story. At the time, he'd been lucky to have escaped with a mild concussion and a few cracked ribs. His cell phone and wallet had been the least of his worries. "I know it's not an excuse, but I didn't get your messages. See? New phone, new number."

She stared at him with wide, solemn blue eyes. "You had a right to know about the babies, but please understand that, other than some financial support, I don't expect anything from you."

He scowled, annoyed with the way the conversation was going. "What do you mean? I'm their father."

Her unblinking gaze bored into his. "Can you honestly tell me you're here to stay this time? That you'll be here for me and the babies no matter what? You'll never need to take another unexpected personal leave of absence?"

For long moments he debated lying to her and reassuring her he was here to stay. But his life wasn't his own. He had responsibilities. If his mother called, he'd have to drop everything to leave again.

And he couldn't lie to Alyssa, even by omission.

Not about this.

"No, I can't tell you that I won't ever leave Cedar Bluff. But if I do have to leave, I'll make sure to let you know first. And you can rest assured that, no matter what happens, I have every intention of being there to help support you and the twins. Emotionally support them, as well as financially."

Her eyes widened in surprise, as if she hadn't expected him to say that. "But you made it clear you weren't interested in a serious relationship," she protested, her eyes full of barely hidden anxiety.

"So did you," he shot back.

She stared at him, unable to refute his claim. They'd blithely jumped into an intimate relationship, never considering the possible consequences of their actions.

"Obviously things have changed, for both of us," Jadon continued. "I plan to be a part of my children's lives, so you'd better get used to the idea." She wasn't going to get rid of him that easily. "I'll give you some space now, because I don't want to cause you any more stress while you're supposed to be resting, but you can be certain I'll be back later."

She didn't utter a word as he turned and walked away.

CHAPTER THREE

ALYSSA had no idea bed rest could be so boring. It seemed all she could think about were the things she couldn't do. The next twenty-four hours crawled by painfully slowly. Daytime television was pathetic. She searched and searched for some Christmas-themed programs but didn't find a single one. Where were all the wonderful Christmas shows she'd remembered watching as a kid? Didn't they air them anymore?

She hoped the hospital carolers would come back. Or maybe the music channel on the television? She picked up the remote and turned it on, taking a deep breath when the lyrical sound of Christmas music filled the air.

She closed her eyes and hummed along, trying not to dwell on the four hospital walls holding her captive.

The problem with having nothing to do was that her thoughts kept going back to Jadon. He hadn't made good on his threat to return, and she wasn't certain if she was relieved by the lapse or disappointed. She tried to convince herself his absence was for the best. She needed time to get over the shock of knowing he was back. Somehow, she simply couldn't believe he'd meant what he'd said.

He wanted to be a part of their children's lives? Supporting them emotionally as well as financially? What exactly did that mean?

Was he envisioning some sort of joint custody agreement? Dual parenting? The thought of giving up her babies on alternate weekends made her feel sick.

So she tried not to think about their dubious future at all. Especially since Jadon hadn't been able to promise he wouldn't leave again. Maybe his definition of emotional support was different from hers. Once he understood the amount of work twins entailed, he'd likely disappear for good, just like her father had. She needed to keep her heart safe. No way did she want to be hurt like that again.

Several of her coworkers stopped by to see her, giving the occasional break in the monotony. Susan, her coworker in the ED, brought her a beautiful red poinsettia plant, which provided a cheerful, festive feeling to her room. Seth had popped in very briefly to assure her that Ben was indeed doing fine and that he'd be discharged the following morning.

Alyssa could only hope an early morning discharge was in her future, too.

As she hadn't done a thing all day except lie in bed watching television, sleep didn't come easily. She spent far too much time thinking of Jadon.

Remembering their last night together.

The way they'd made love, urgently, as if knowing, instinctively, the heat and passion between them couldn't last.

The desolation she'd felt once she'd realized he was gone.

At the time, she'd told herself she was better off without him. They'd met during a very complicated trauma resuscitation, two victims of a multiple motor-vehicle crash. From the very beginning, she'd realized Jadon was an excellent physician. She'd admired the way he kept calm in a crisis, yet treated the distraught families with dignity and respect. His charisma was like a beacon, drawing her near. She'd warned herself to ignore the attraction she felt for him, but it seemed like every time she glanced up at him, he was staring at her.

When their fingers had touched that first time, pure electricity had sizzled between them.

Eventually, they weren't able to stay away from each other. He asked her to come home with him after a late shift they'd shared, and against her better judgment she agreed.

She knew better than to fall for a handsome guy like Jadon. Her mother had harped on the inability of handsome men to remain faithful. Alyssa had seen a few of the early photographs of her parents together, realizing her father had indeed been a good-looking guy.

And he'd left a week before her third birthday, leaving her mother to raise a young daughter all alone.

All her life Alyssa had tried to avoid ending up like her mother. Her mother had been forced to go from job to job, always seeking better pay, which hadn't been easy since she didn't have a college degree or any specialty training. It wasn't her mother's fault that she'd spent more time working, or obsessing about working, than paying attention to Alyssa.

So Alyssa had vowed to make something of her life.

To never be dependent on any man. She'd taken out student loans to attend college, to have a career as an ED nurse so she'd never have to worry about not having a steady, reliable job.

She'd also avoided being hurt by men, like her mother had been, keeping her relationships light-hearted and fun. Especially if the guy she was with seemed like he wasn't exactly father material.

Like Jadon. Yet here she was, pregnant and alone. With twins, which put a big crimp in her plan to stay independent.

And as much as she wanted to blame Jadon, she knew the truth of the matter was that she had no one to blame for her situation but herself.

Jadon was exhausted; he'd been called in early for his night shift because the ED had been flooded with trauma calls. He hadn't slept very well in the first place, and being called in early meant he'd missed going back up to L & D to check on Alyssa. During the night, he'd had a few minutes of downtime, but obviously then wasn't the appropriate time to wake her.

When he finished his shift at eight-thirty in the morning, he took a few minutes to swing by to see how she was doing.

He helped himself to more coffee, double-strength to keep the fatigue at bay. With less than three hours of sleep, and a physically demanding endless stream of patients, his entire body ached, as if he'd been run over by an eighteen-wheeler.

As he stepped off the elevators on the fifth floor labor and delivery area, he ran into Seth, Kylie and

Ben. He quickly realized they were making their way down to see Alyssa as well.

"Jadon," Seth greeted him coolly. The silence stretched for a long moment before Seth grudgingly made formal introductions. "This is my fiancée, Kylie Germaine. And her son, soon to be our son, Ben. Kylie and Ben, this is Dr. Jadon Reichert, one of the ED physicians here at Cedar Bluff."

"Good to see you both again," Jadon said, forcing a smile. He'd noticed Seth hadn't introduced him as a friend, but only as a colleague. He turned his attention to the boy. "Especially you, Ben. You're doing much better than yesterday."

"Yes, well, he's finally been discharged, but has also refused to leave without seeing Alyssa," Kylie commented dryly.

"Alyssa can't come to visit me because she might have her babies too early," Ben announced in an all-important tone.

Jadon's lips twitched with the need to grin. "Yes, that's right," he agreed. "She needs to rest. But I know she'll be glad to see you, as she's been very worried about you."

"I love Alyssa," Ben said very seriously. "She risked her life for me."

"I think she's special, too," Jadon said, his chest feeling tight with emotion. He thought Ben's case of hero worship for Alyssa was sweet. Not that he blamed the kid.

He'd heard the story yesterday, about how Alyssa had fallen into the icy water, trying to rescue Ben. She'd gotten the boy out first, but then almost couldn't make her way out of the water. When he thought of how things could have ended very differently, he felt sick and shaky all over.

"Come on, Ben," Seth said, interrupting them. "Let's go and visit Alyssa, shall we?"

Jadon told himself he was overreacting to Seth's abruptness, but the way Kylie dodged his gaze only confirmed it wasn't his imagination. With a flash of annoyance he tried not to obsess about how he didn't even know Kylie on a personal level—she hadn't been here in Cedar Bluff when he'd left—so there was no reason for her to carry a grudge against him. She'd obviously picked up on Seth's disdain.

Part of their attitude might be because they were afraid he'd leave Alyssa again, he acknowledged.

But even more, he suspected Seth didn't think he was good enough for Alyssa. A fact he couldn't argue.

Even aside from the problem of sustaining a relationship, what did he know about being a father? Or having a normal family? Nothing. His family had been anything but normal.

He stood where he was, watching them make their way down the hall to Alyssa's room, a closely knit family unit, regardless of the lack of formality of marriage. Clearly they were good friends with Alyssa.

Maybe this wasn't a good time to visit after all. His presence in the room with Seth, Kylie and Ben would only make things awkward.

Coward, his subconscious jeered.

With a muttered oath he continued down the hall to Alyssa's room. He stood in the doorway, watching her smile and laugh while hugging Ben.

He swallowed the hard lump in his throat and stepped farther in the room.

When Alyssa saw him, the light in her eyes dimmed. "Hi, Jadon."

"How are you feeling?" he asked, avoiding Seth's none-too-subtle glare. "You look much better this morning."

"I am better," Alyssa said. "Dr. Rayborn has written my discharge notice. I'm free to go home."

"That's wonderful news." He was very glad to realize that Alyssa was stable enough to go home. At least he didn't have to worry about the twins being born too prematurely.

"I have to stay on bed rest for a few days," Alyssa explained, including all of them in her earnest gaze. "But Dr. Rayborn told me to come back to see her on Wednesday. If all goes well, I might be able to return to work after that."

He bit back a protest, knowing his opinion on her working this late in her pregnancy wouldn't be welcome. He wanted to reassure her about how he planned to help her to financially support the babies but at the same time he didn't want to invite an argument, especially in front of Seth and Kylie.

"Don't rush things," Kylie warned, and he wanted to kiss her in gratitude for saying exactly what he was thinking. "Remember, stay healthy so you can carry those babies to term."

"I know. I've already heard the same lecture from Dr. Rayborn," Alyssa protested, holding up a hand with a wry smile. "I won't rush things, but you know as well as I do that the longer I work before the delivery, the more time I can take off after the twins are born."

Again, Jadon had to bite his tongue to keep from interrupting. If he had his way, Alyssa wouldn't have to work for a long time after the twins were born. He might not know much about being a father, but he refused to let her struggle to make ends meet either.

Yet he understood they had a long way to go before she'd lean on him. So he'd be patient, taking one day at a time.

"Do you need a ride home?" Seth asked. "We're happy to stop by your place since Ben's officially discharged, too."

"That would be great," Alyssa said gratefully. "The nurses have already done the discharge teaching. All I need is a prescription for the oral terbutaline Dr. Rayborn wants me to continue taking and I'll be ready to go."

Jadon frowned, thinking her condition didn't sound too stable to him. "I can give you a ride home, Alyssa. That way Kylie and Seth don't have to wait."

Seth flashed a grim smile, crossed his arms over his chest. "Oh, it's no bother. We don't mind waiting, do we, Kylie? And besides, you worked graveyard last night, didn't you? I heard the ED was crazy. Might be better for you to hurry home and get some sleep. You look exhausted."

The dismissive note in Seth's tone put Jadon's teeth on edge. Silently, Jadon glanced at Alyssa, giving her the final word. She hesitated, and then grimaced as she nodded. "Jadon, I didn't realize you've just finished working the night shift. I'll go home with Kylie and Seth. You do look like you could use some sleep."

Her choice to go with her friends, rather than with him,

stung. Maybe he'd made mistakes but, dammit, it wasn't all his fault. He hadn't left knowing Alyssa was pregnant.

When the nurse didn't immediately return with Alyssa's prescription, he knew he'd lost the battle. Swallowing a heavy sigh, he turned and left, trying to be happy that Alyssa was doing well enough to go home.

But if she thought she could avoid him forever, she was wrong. Maybe he did need some sleep, but he and Alyssa needed to talk. Soon.

Preferably without an audience.

Alyssa sat on her sofa, staring morosely at her crooked Charlie Brown Christmas tree standing in the living-room corner of her apartment. She'd thought the ornaments would help fill in the sparse gaps between the branches, but instead the branches slumped beneath the weight of even her smallest ornaments.

Her apartment manager, Mr. Worthington, had brought her the tree and hauled her ornament boxes out of her storage bin located in the basement. Mr. Worthington was a sweet man; he'd been a devoted fan ever since the night he'd had crushing chest pain and she'd stayed by his side during the ambulance ride to the hospital.

So she couldn't complain about the tree. Instead, she should be glad she had at least something Christmassy to look at. Christmas had always been her favorite holiday even while she'd been growing up. It had been the one time of the year when her mother had gone all out, lots of decorations and celebrating to make their time together special. In recent years, though, since her mother had passed away, the holiday spirit had been more difficult to find. Now, with the babies coming, she'd grown excited about Christmas again.

However, bed rest did not include putting up Christmas decorations, or baking Christmas cookies. Heck, she couldn't even scrub the floors or really do anything to relieve the boredom of her apartment.

When the doorbell buzzed, indicating she had a visitor, she crossed over to the intercom system, expecting her coworker from the ED. "Susan? Is that you?"

"No. It's Jadon."

Alyssa closed her eyes and momentarily rested her forehead on the wall. She'd known Jadon wouldn't leave her alone for long, especially after she'd turned down a ride with him earlier that morning. She'd seen the flash of hurt in his eyes when she'd agreed to go home with Seth. She'd felt guilty.

But she wasn't any more ready to continue their discussion now than she had been earlier in the day.

Since avoiding him hadn't worked, she pushed the button to release the door lock of the apartment. In moments he knocked on her door.

She ran her fingers through her hair and opened it, all too aware of how awful she looked wearing maternity sweats. Not that she should care.

But she did.

"Alyssa, are you supposed to be up off the sofa?" he asked, his brow furrowed with concern as he shut the door behind him.

She suppressed a sigh, telling herself it was natural he was worried about the babies. They were his babies, too.

"Yes, I can make simple meals for myself, walk to

the bathroom and back. I'm to keep a log of any contractions I have and to call Dr. Rayborn if they become at all regular or sustained."

Jadon nodded and thrust his hands deep into his pockets. "I'm glad. Kim seems like a great doctor."

"Yes, she is." Alyssa made her way back to the sofa. "Help yourself if you want something to drink."

"I'm fine." Jadon followed her into the living room, taking a seat on the chair across from her. If he noticed her pathetic little Christmas tree, he didn't say anything. "Alyssa, I'm sorry. I shouldn't have left all those months ago without saying anything. Give me a chance to explain."

She swallowed hard and shook her head. "Jadon, if this story involves some other woman, like an ex-wife, a fiancée or a girlfriend, I really don't want to hear the gory details."

"What?" His startled expression would have been comical if she hadn't felt sick to her stomach to be having this confrontation. "Is that really what you think? That I left you for some other woman?"

She rubbed a hand over her stomach, hoping she could calm the babies, sheltering them from her tension. "What was I supposed to think? Why else would you leave without a word?"

"There isn't another woman, Alyssa. Not now, or during the time we were together." His low tone and the seriousness in his gaze made it difficult to doubt him. "But you're right, I haven't been entirely truthful with you. About my past."

She licked suddenly dry lips, suspecting she wasn't going to like this. "To be fair, Jadon, neither one of us talked much about our pasts." Their physical attraction had overridden most of the normal let's-get-to-know-each-other small talk.

"Alyssa, I left Cedar Bluff a few months ago because of a family crisis."

"A family crisis? One of your parents?" she asked in concern, remembering the few sketchy details they'd shared about their backgrounds.

Slowly he shook his head, letting out a heavy sigh. "They're fine, well, sort of, but that wasn't the problem. It was my brother who needed help. I know this isn't fair, but I'd rather not go into all the details right now because it's complicated."

"Complicated," she repeated, trying not to feel hurt. She tried to tell herself that whatever had happened wasn't her business, but it was difficult. "I guess I can understand." Even though she really didn't. Then again, she shouldn't be surprised. Jadon had always tried to keep his distance from her emotionally. This was just another example.

"I'll tell you the entire story sometime, but right now I'm more worried about you. And the babies."

"There isn't anything to be worried about. I'm fine and so are the twins." She gave a small shrug, hiding her true feelings. Jadon had never confided in her before, and obviously he didn't see a reason to start now. Maybe he hadn't left her for another woman, but that didn't change the fact that he wasn't open to a future. "All I can do is follow doctor's orders and hope for the best."

"Yes. But I'd really like to help."

"Help?" she repeated, trying to figure out where he

was going with this. "Like with what? The babies haven't been born yet."

"Do you have everything you need?" he asked. "It's going to be rough as you need two of everything. So what about cribs? Car seats? Strollers?"

The thought of Jadon buying baby things almost made her smile. "Seth and Kylie threw me a shower, inviting all the ED staff, so I have most of what I need, thanks."

He swept a skeptical glance over her apartment. "You'll be crowded in here, don't you think?"

She raised a brow. "For now maybe we'll be a little cramped. But I won't be living here forever." At least, that was her plan. She had some small savings that she hoped to use as a down payment for a house, depending on how things went after the twins were born. If she could work enough hours to afford a small mortgage.

"Alyssa, I have a three-bedroom house. There's no reason you can't move in with me for the rest of your pregnancy and then even after the babies are born. Between the two of us, we should be able to help care for the twins, keeping our child-care costs down."

Her eyes widened in shock. Was he crazy? Was he really suggesting they live together for financial reasons? As if the babies were nothing more than a business arrangement? "I don't think that's a good idea."

In fact, she was pretty sure it was a really bad idea. His emotions may not be involved, but hers would be.

"Please, think about it." He didn't back down as she half expected he might, but stood awkwardly in her living room, looking like a fish out of water. "I know things have been rough for you, and I'm sorry you had to go through this alone. But right now we need to focus on the babies. Having you move in with me, even temporarily, is best for them."

CHAPTER FOUR

LONG after Jadon had left, Alyssa found herself replaying their brief conversation over and over again.

He'd asked her to move in with him. As a business arrangement. Because there was extra room in his three-bedroom house. A temporary solution to solve her child-care needs.

Typical of Jadon to gloss over the emotional side of things. Did he ever think about their time together? Did he have any feelings for her at all? Other than as the mother of his children? Children he'd never planned on having?

Logically, she knew his offer had some merit. She'd always sworn not to end up like her mother, struggling to make ends meet. And now here was Jadon, offering a solution to at least part of her problems. But at what cost?

Emotionally, sharing a roof with Jadon would risk her heart, a huge price to pay.

Yet didn't her babies deserve a safe and secure childhood? And would she really be able to provide that on her own? For one baby, yes, but for two? Doubtful.

She hadn't given him an answer, simply telling him she'd need to think about it.

For a long time she stared at the pretty, bright star

topping her lopsided Christmas tree, as if seeking divine guidance. What on earth should she do? Maybe moving in with him would be best for the twins, but what about her?

If only her pulse didn't leap so erratically whenever Jadon was nearby. If only she didn't still feel that spark of attraction whenever he spoke to her. If only she didn't wish so much that things were different.

She'd gone into a relationship with Jadon planning to keep things light, but she'd been hurt more than she'd realized when he'd left. Maybe he'd left for a family crisis but, still, he hadn't called to let her know he was coming back. Clearly he hadn't anticipated renewing their relationship. Because they hadn't *had* a relationship.

She didn't want to be hurt again. Jadon had already proved himself to be too much like her father. She'd be better off to stay away from him.

Except he was the father of her babies.

Avoiding him would be impossible. Somehow she had to find a way to work with Jadon, to meet the needs of her children, without becoming emotionally dependent on him.

Could she do it? Live with him as a business arrangement, to help share the trials of providing feedings for two infants every two to three hours, without getting emotionally involved?

The four walls of her apartment were closing in on her, especially the way she couldn't do anything. She longed to leave. Yet the idea of moving in with Jadon seemed too much like simply exchanging one type of prison for another.

* * *

Jadon figured he'd botched things with Alyssa for good. He hadn't intended to bring up them moving in together, yet suddenly it had seemed like such a great idea. Obviously, by her horrified expression, she hadn't shared his enthusiasm.

And her wishy-washy, gee-let-me-think-about-it response hadn't been promising.

Seeing Alyssa in her cramped apartment, with her crooked Christmas tree, had bothered him. He couldn't imagine how she'd possibly take care of two babies in the single-bedroom apartment. Especially as she didn't have anyone to lean on for support. Her mother had passed away a few years ago and she was an only child.

The rest of Alyssa's past was sketchy. He knew she was estranged from her father, but that was about it. They hadn't made an attempt to know each other on a deeply personal level.

Their relationship had been physically intimate. He'd realized how much he was starting to care for her at the same time his family crisis had torn him away. He'd thought the distance would help.

But he'd missed her. Had thought about her a lot. Had missed their physical closeness.

A closeness he'd considered resuming once he'd returned, since he'd learned a lot about his brother's illness while he'd been gone. He'd spent time with Jack's doctor, who'd put some of his old fears to rest.

And, truthfully, he'd liked their hot, steamy nights together.

Alyssa's pregnancy changed everything. He didn't know anything about being a father. The idea of raising children, twins on top of it, secretly scared him. He knew, only too well, how things could go wrong.

With a sigh, he rubbed his aching temple and then decided to head for the shower. He was on for another night shift tonight, then had only one day off before working again on Wednesday night. At least he had Thursday and Friday off before being back on for the weekend. He'd been assigned the less-desirable grave-yard shifts and weekends, but since the physician team had covered for him while he'd been gone for the past four and a half months, he couldn't exactly complain.

Even though he personally would have rather stayed here, he understood there were feelings of resentment among the others.

Simon Carter had been pretty decent toward him. And there was a new guy, Quinn Torres, scheduled to start soon, to replace Ed Cagney, who'd just retired. But Seth Taylor had been another story. Seth couldn't have made his feelings any clearer.

Monday night started out fairly quiet. He had to admit he was glad of the chance to ease back into the work he'd loved and hadn't been able to do for so long.

At midnight, a woman carrying a small infant rushed in.

"He aspirated and started turning blue." The woman was talking fast, but with the way she used medical ter-minology, he thought she was probably a doctor or a nurse. "I didn't do any CPR, but used the bulb suction to keep his airway cleared."

"Okay, let's take a look." They must not have called

911, but had driven here themselves. He reached for his peds stethoscope. "How old is the baby?"

"Ten days old." Her voice shook as he gently took the baby and placed him on the infant table. Melanie, one of the nurses, placed a pulse-ox device on his forehead and then stripped off his little outfit to put tiny EKG patches on his chest.

"Pulse ox 86 percent," Melanie said in a low tone. She fiddled with the heart monitor. "Heart rate 176."

He nodded and used his stethoscope to listen to the little guy's lungs. He definitely must have aspirated as Jadon could hear rales in the bases of his lungs.

"Did you witness the aspiration?" he asked the visibly upset mother.

She nodded. "It was my fault. All my fault. I had him propped on his side after his feeding, but I couldn't have tucked the blanket securely enough behind his body. Next thing I know, he's lying on his back, turning blue." She momentarily closed her eyes. "It was awful."

He gave her a reassuring smile. "Well, his pulse ox is coming back up, he's almost at 90 percent. And his heart rate was pretty tachy, but that's coming down, too. So far he's not running a fever, but that probably won't happen until tomorrow. Who's your pediatrician?"

"Dr. Piterle, in the Pediatric Care Group."

Jadon gave Melanie a nod and she left to get in touch with whichever pediatrician in the group happened to be on call. "Are you a nurse?"

"Yes, although I haven't worked since having my daughter."

"I thought so. What's your son's name? We need to get him admitted into the system."

"Never mind, Dr. Reichert." Wendy, the night shift

admitting clerk, came into the room. "Dad's here and gave us all the information we need. This little guy is Aiden Crosby."

"My name is Diane and my husband is Steve." Diane introduced her husband, who came into the room with a cute toddler in his arms. "And my daughter, Katie."

Melanie returned. "Dr. Piterle was on call and he didn't think Aiden needed to spend the night, but he does want to follow up with the baby tomorrow morning."

Diane nodded with relief. "Okay, that's fine."

"Now, remember, if he runs a fever tomorrow, he'll probably need a full course of antibiotics," Jadon warned. "IV antibiotics since he's so young. But for now his pulse ox and heart rate are back to normal, so he should be in the clear."

"Thank you," Diane said gratefully.

Jadon was glad the ten-day-old Aiden would be all right, but seeing the tiny baby only made him think about Alyssa and their twins. He was more convinced than ever that it would be best for her to move in with him. He took his responsibilities seriously. He needed to convince Alyssa to let him support her.

In the morning, he decided to stop at the grocery store for her, since she obviously couldn't do it on her own. Rather than guess what she wanted to eat, he headed over to her apartment to get a list.

But when he pulled up, he saw Kylie, Seth and Ben hauling some grocery bags out of their car and trooping up to Alyssa's apartment building. He was too late.

Alyssa didn't really need him after all.

* * *

The ED was unusually quiet on Wednesday night when he entered the arena. When Jadon saw Alyssa standing near Susan, the charge nurse assigned to the night shift, discussing the various patient assignments, he was shocked.

How was it possible she was back at work already? Sure, she'd mentioned something about only being on bed rest for a few days and being scheduled to see Kim Rayborn today, but to already be released to work? It had to be too soon.

What if she started having contractions again?

"Hi, Alyssa," he greeted her, careful to keep his tone light. "I see you're back at work."

"Jadon." Her smile was fleeting. "It feels good to be back. I was going crazy sitting at home."

He nodded, barely refraining from pointing out she didn't have to be at her apartment all alone. He'd wanted her with him.

"Who wants to cover the trauma room?" Susan asked.

"I will," Alyssa volunteered. She smiled at the new nurse, Maureen, who was learning the ropes. "Maureen can work with me."

"Okay, I'll put you guys down as first trauma coverage." Susan scribbled on her clipboard.

"Did you see the full moon out there?" Alyssa said to Susan and Maureen. "It was so beautiful."

"Yeah, beautiful." Susan let out a loud snort. "You know what a full moon means—more work for us. The crazies will be out in full force."

"Is that really true?" Maureen asked with wide eyes.

"You bet," Susan said. She turned to Alyssa. "Remember last month, Alyssa? When the police brought us that guy who'd stripped down to his bare butt while standing right in the middle of Main Street? Like, what were we supposed to do with him? Other than put his clothes back on." Susan rolled her eyes at the memory.

Alyssa nodded and let out a chuckle. "Yeah, he was a strange one all right."

Jadon clenched his jaw at their slightly derogatory tone. He wanted to snap at them to shut up because obviously people couldn't help having emotional illnesses, but he also knew they didn't mean any harm. Alyssa and Susan were excellent nurses.

He was just being overly sensitive. He turned away, to focus his attention on the two patients who were still waiting to be transferred up to inpatient floor beds. He needed to make sure these patients were placed before new ones began to arrive.

They received their first trauma call about thirty minutes later, a car versus tree. The driver was a young man who luckily didn't have severe injuries. Jadon and Alyssa fell into a familiar rhythm, working together as if he'd never left. When she handed him a chest tube insertion tray, the slightest brush of her fingers sent an unexpected yet familiar tingle of awareness zipping through his system.

"Thanks," he managed.

The way she avoided his direct gaze convinced him she might have felt it, too. This sizzling attraction had drawn them irrevocably together the first time they'd met. Tonight was proof the passing of time hadn't lessened the attraction.

He still wanted her.

There wasn't time to dwell on the knowledge because as soon as they managed to get the patient stabilized, it was as if a dam had burst, the way the patients flooded in.

Loud screaming erupted from the ED waiting room.

Jadon glanced up in alarm. "Stay here," he told Alyssa as he dashed through the doors into the waiting area to see what was going on.

"Don't touch me! Leave me alone! I can't listen— Don't touch me!"

A man stood in the center of the room, his eyes wild, his clothes disheveled, a three-day growth of beard covering his face. He grabbed at the hair on his head with one hand, while waving a butter knife clutched in the other. While the butter knife wasn't sharp, it could still be used as a weapon and the few people in the waiting room were pressed against the back wall, giving the guy a wide berth.

"Easy, now," Jadon said, waving a hand at the others to indicate everyone should stay back. He prayed Alyssa hadn't followed him in. She was pregnant. He didn't want her anywhere near this guy. "No one is going to touch you. I promise, no one is going to touch you."

"I can't. They won't stop— I can't listen. Don't touch me." The man was clearly in distress, and Jadon knew that if he didn't help this man calm down, he might quickly turn violent.

And violence meant someone would get hurt.

Not Alyssa. Please, keep Alyssa safe from harm.

"No one is going to hurt you. You can relax now. I can help you. You're safe here." Jadon understood, only too well, that while this man seemed crazy, his wild actions were the result of a deep fear.

Fear of what, he wasn't sure. Something the rest of them couldn't see but that was very real to this man, nonetheless.

He continued to talk to the man holding the butter knife in a calm tone, reassuring him he was safe here. No matter how much he wanted to turn around and look for Alyssa, to make sure she was safe, Jadon didn't break eye contact with the patient. And as he continued to talk him down, he hoped the hospital staff, including the security guards, were busy getting the other patients and their families out of the waiting room, just in case.

Psych crisis de-escalation techniques didn't always work the way they were intended to. It paid to be prepared for anything.

"I'm here to help you. You're safe here. My name is Jadon. What's yours?"

"Mitch. Mitchell Park Conservatory. I'm Mitch, but I'm not crazy. I don't have to listen."

Jadon wasn't sure if this guy's name was really Mitch or not, as the Mitchell Park Conservatory was actually three horticultural domes that served as a local tourist attraction in Milwaukee, but he decided to go with it. "It's nice to meet you, Mitch. You're here in the safe zone where no one can hurt you. It's my job to keep you safe. You're not crazy. I think you're scared. But you don't have to be afraid. You're safe with me."

The more he repeated himself, and key phrases like *You're safe here with me*, the better chance he had of convincing Mitch to calm down enough to let go of the butter knife. Jadon suspected Mitch was suffering from some form of schizophrenia, especially if he was really hearing voices in his head.

He wanted to hurry and get the guy some treatment, but rushing him would only make things worse, so he forced himself to take his time, to remain calm and to keep his gaze trained on Mitch, hyperaware of his every movement.

It took him nearly twenty minutes, but Mitch eventually gave up his knife and agreed to go into an examination room. Jadon steered him toward the opposite end of the emergency department where they could isolate him to a certain extent from the other patients.

"Nice job," Alyssa said in a quiet voice, once he'd given Mitch a mild sedative, a similar dose, they'd discovered in going through his old records, to the one that he should have been taking at home.

"Thanks. I'm glad you stayed far away," he admitted.

She frowned. "Of course. I'm not stupid."

He winced. "I didn't mean to say you were. I was just worried about you."

Alyssa stared at him for a long moment and he wanted to pull her close and kiss her, but they didn't have that kind of relationship. Not anymore. Finally she turned away and he heard her calling the psych crisis center for Mitch.

"See?" he heard Susan say to Maureen. "You thought we were kidding, didn't you? I told you the crazies would be out. Mitch is a true nutcase."

Her derogatory tone caused him to spin around, pinning her with a fierce glare. "He's not crazy, he's sick," he said in a low, furious tone. "His illness isn't any different from having diabetes or congestive heart failure. And I don't want to hear you call him a nutcase again, do you understand?"

Susan's eyes widened and she took a hasty step back, making him irritated all over again, especially when he realized Alyssa was staring at him with troubled concern. "Sure. I'm sorry, Dr. Reichert."

Only slightly mollified, he turned away, continuing to see patients one after the other as the full moon kept its promise of keeping them busy.

Mitch had brought all Jadon's old fears to the surface. He should stay far away from Alyssa, yet he couldn't make himself. When he realized he was creating excuses to be near her, he knew Mitch wasn't the crazy one.

He was.

Because it was crazy to want something he could never have.

CHAPTER FIVE

ALYSSA waited patiently until the respiratory therapist finished giving Mr. Waverly a breathing treatment for his pneumonia, then she placed the peripheral IV he required for his full course of antibiotics.

She couldn't help wondering about Jadon while she worked. It was very unusual for him to snap at anyone the way he'd jumped on Susan. In fact, she'd never seen him as uptight as he'd been during this shift.

Although facing wild Mitch who'd been armed with a butter knife would put anyone on edge.

Had he always been somewhat protective of patients with emotional illnesses? She thought back to those first few weeks they'd worked together, but couldn't really remember.

Ashamed, she realized she hadn't taken the time to really understand Jadon. She'd settled for a physically intimate relationship, enjoying the sheer thrill of being with him. And working with him tonight brought the intense feelings of attraction back again. She was aware of him at every moment. It was hard to concentrate when he was near. Yet she also missed him when he was gone.

When he'd left, she'd been upset because she'd started falling for him, even though she'd told herself she wouldn't, and then later because she'd discovered she was pregnant.

The latter was her fault—to a certain extent—as much as his.

A mere touch from Jadon while they were caring for their patients made her remember the hours they'd spent together making love. Yet there was so much about him she didn't know. Who was Jadon, really? And what past experiences had molded him into the man he'd become?

Ironic that she knew as much about Jadon as she did about her long-absent father.

They'd become intimate, agreeing they weren't looking for a long-term relationship, but here they were, about to be parents of twins. What a tangled mess.

She put her troubled thoughts aside, refusing to allow her personal life to interfere with her professional one. As the night wore on, Alyssa became more and more fatigued. There wasn't much downtime during the night thanks to the full moon hanging over the hospital like a large, yellow-orange bad-luck charm.

She started Mr. Waverly's antibiotics as Jadon had ordered for his pneumonia and stifled a yawn as she trudged slowly back to the main desk. Every room was full and she knew there would undoubtedly be additional patients assigned to her.

"Alyssa, take a break," Jadon murmured in a low tone as he came up behind her. "Put your feet up and relax for a bit."

Jadon's concern was touching, but she shook her head. "There are still patients who've been waiting almost two hours to be seen. I'll take a break once we've gotten caught up." Which, at the rate they were going, might be never.

"Alyssa, please." He put his hand on her arm, stopping her from walking away. "Maureen can cover for a bit."

She looked at his strong hand and wished he'd cared as much about her before she'd become pregnant, and was now not just focused on the babies. She missed being held by him more than she'd realized.

"Soon," she said, regretfully pulling away. She missed the warmth of his hand when it dropped to his side.

She only had to hang on a few more hours as the oncoming shift started at seven in the morning, yet she also knew that if there were still lots of patients she couldn't just leave when her shift was up.

A trauma call came in at five forty-five in the morning, giving her a badly needed spurt of adrenaline. A young twenty-one-year-old man had fallen asleep at the wheel, crossed the center line and hit an oncoming car. The woman in the other vehicle was in her mid-forties, and had been having significant abdominal pain at the scene of the crash. The airbag had saved her from a serious head injury, thank heavens.

"Get a trauma surgeon down here," Jadon ordered. He glanced at Alyssa. "I want to know her hematocrit and hemoglobin. I suspect she's ruptured her spleen, bleeding into her belly."

Alyssa nodded. She quickly finished her initial set of vitals and then proceeded to draw the labs he'd requested. She handed them to the runner and then turned back to her patient. The woman's name was Elaine Sansone, and the way she moaned in pain on the gurney made Alyssa privately agree with Jadon's assessment. Elanie's abdomen was hard and painful to the touch.

"I need a CT scan of her belly stat. Where the heck is Trauma Surgery?"

"I'm here," Leila Ross said, entering the trauma bay. She was a petite woman with exotic Oriental features and beautiful straight long black hair. "What do you have?"

Alyssa continued checking Elaine's vital signs, not entirely surprised when her blood pressure dropped dramatically, confirming Jadon's assessment of bleeding into her belly. "Blood pressure is down to ninety systolic. Do you want me to give more fluid?" she asked.

Jadon nodded. "Give a liter bolus of normal saline. Leila? What do you want to do?"

"A CT scan would help, but if her pressure is that low, I think it's better if we simply take her up to the OR. I can explore her belly up there."

"Alyssa?" Jadon glanced at her. "Get Elaine transferred up to the OR."

"What about the other patient?" The young twenty-one-year-old, by the name of Curt Neilson, had suffered multiple fractures, especially in his forearms and his right leg. His injuries weren't as critical, so she'd allowed Maureen to handle his care.

"I'm sending him for a slew of radiology films. The orthosurgeon is on his way in. There isn't much more we can do other than manage his pain."

Alyssa nodded and began to connect Elaine to the

portable monitor so she could transport her to the OR. Leila jumped in to assist and between the two of them they wheeled Elaine up to the OR suites. When the OR nurse took over, Alyssa returned to the ED to help Maureen.

It took a while to get Curt's X-rays but just as they finished and returned to the trauma bay, he lost his blood pressure, too. But on the monitor his heart rate still looked as if it was doing all right.

"Check his pulse," Alyssa said sharply.

Maureen put her fingers on his carotid artery, her eyes wide. "I don't feel anything."

Alyssa muttered a curse under her breath and double-checked for herself, although she suspected he was in PEA. "Start CPR," she told Maureen. Raising her voice, she called, "Jadon? We need your help over here."

Jadon rushed over and immediately knew what was going on. "His last set of labs were fine, right?" he asked.

Alyssa nodded. "He does have cracked ribs. Do you think he has a tension pneumothorax?"

"Stop CPR." Jadon picked up an eighteen-gauge needle and inserted it in Curt's fourth and fifth intercostal space. Within moments his pulse returned.

Maureen's eyes were wide. "Wow. It worked. It really worked."

"Yes, it did," Alyssa said in relief. A tension pneumothorax was life-threatening, yet also relatively simple to treat, once you had the correct diagnosis. A glance at the clock told her the day shift would be coming in soon. Thank heavens.

"I love this job," Maureen said reverently.

Alyssa had to laugh. Normally, she loved it, too.

Most of the time. She'd love it tonight if she weren't so darned tired.

They waited a long time for Curt to be accepted as an ICU admission. Once she and Maureen wheeled him upstairs and handed over his care to the ICU team, they were pretty much free to go.

Alyssa punched out at the time clock, and then headed into the staff lounge for a few moments. Whoever had hung the Christmas decorations must have gotten interrupted halfway through. There was red garland strung along the ceiling, but an artificial tree stood in the corner, bare of any ornaments. If she had the energy she'd finish the decorations herself.

Her feet ached terribly, so she plopped in a chair and lifted them up on the table. The soreness in her legs eased and she leaned her head back with a sigh and closed her eyes. She longed to rest, for just a few minutes.

"Alyssa?"

She pried her eyes open, surprised to see Jadon. For a moment she was confused. Where was she? Then she remembered that she'd sat in the staff lounge for a few moments before heading home. "I'm awake," she said, wincing a little as she set her feet back on the floor.

"You're exhausted," Jadon said mildly. "You'd better let me drive you home."

"I'm fine," she protested. "I didn't mean to fall asleep, it's just the first time I've sat down in hours. And I'm more tired these days than usual."

"I know." Jadon's grim gaze met hers. "You earned the right to rest, Alyssa. Heck, I was surprised to see you back at work tonight anyway. Please let me drive you home. It's been snowing for the past hour. You don't want to end up like Curt and Elaine, do you?"

He was right, she was exhausted. But she didn't live that far from the hospital. "They were on the highway," she stubbornly reminded him. "They crashed at high speeds. Different situation altogether."

"A crash is still a crash, regardless. And it doesn't matter, because I'm not taking no for an answer," Jadon said firmly. He bent to take her hand, helping her to her feet. "Come on. It's no trouble. Much better to be safe than sorry."

She gave in, knowing that arguing with Jadon was useless. He was as obstinate as a mule when he wanted to be. That was one area where they'd butted heads in the past—each of them liked having their own way. But for now she was too tired to argue anyway, so she reached for her coat, surprised when Jadon took it from her grasp and held it for her.

"Thanks," she murmured.

Outside, snow fell from the sky in large, thick flakes. An inch of fresh snow covered the ground, and she knew the roads would be slippery.

Much better choice to sit back and let Jadon drive.

"In you go," he said, opening the passenger door of his car and helping her in. Her stomach tended to get in the way, so she backed into the seat and then swung her legs around.

Jadon tucked her in, closed the door behind her and then slid into the driver's seat. He started the car and then went back out to brush the snow away from the windows.

Shivering a little, Alyssa huddled in her coat, remembering how cold she'd been the afternoon she'd fallen into Lake Michigan. At times like this the cold seemed to seep into her bones, making her wonder if she'd ever be warm again.

She'd always been warm in Jadon's arms, she thought with a sigh, putting her head back and closing her eyes.

Somewhere along the route home she fell asleep. When Jadon gently shook her, she lifted her heavy eyelids, blinking against the bright snow. "Where are we?"

"My house. Don't argue. Two cars were sitting sideways in the road leading to your apartment complex because the hill was too slick for them to make it up, so I came here instead."

She let out a heavy breath. "I don't want to argue, but I hate to cause trouble," she said weakly.

He sent her a narrow glare. "Don't be silly. You're no trouble, Alyssa. At least here I can keep an eye on you."

An eye on her for what? Because she needed a caretaker? At least before they'd been equal partners in their intimacy. Now he was treating her more like a responsibility.

She didn't like it. She wanted to mean more.

"Wait for me. The driveway is very icy."

Since she couldn't lever herself out of the car without help anyway, she waited. Jadon tugged her out of the car, and then wrapped his arm around her waist, supporting her as they gingerly made their way across the slick, snowy sidewalk up to the house.

This close to him, his familiar musky scent filled her head, bringing back memories of the nights they'd spent together. Did he think about those times at all?

She glanced up at him as he unlocked the door, ir-rationally wishing she could force him to remember. Large, fluffy snowflakes covered his dark hair, cling-ing to his eyelashes. For a moment their gazes locked and she could tell their closeness affected him, too. But then he stepped back, helping to take her coat off as if she couldn't perform the simple task herself. And suddenly she wanted to prove she wasn't weak or help-less.

"Jadon." He froze when she placed a hand on the middle of his chest. His eyes darkened and his heart beat erratically beneath her fingertips and she knew she finally had his full attention. Keeping her gaze locked on his, she gripped his shirt, lifted herself up on her toes and pressed her mouth against his.

Stunned, Jadon couldn't move, absorbing the heady taste of her kiss. The intense heat that simmered beneath the surface didn't take long to ignite and within moments he'd clutched her close, her round belly pressed intimately against him as he deepened the kiss.

She tasted so sweet, he couldn't get enough. How long had it been since he'd touched her? Held her? It seemed like forever.

"Jadon," she whispered on a moan, and suddenly he realized what he was doing. This couldn't happen. He broke off the kiss, breathing heavily.

"I'm sorry," he muttered, trying to regain his equi-librium. "I shouldn't have done that."

Alyssa stared at him with an oddly hurt expression. "I'm the one who kissed you."

She had, and he wasn't sure why. Unless she was

under the delusion they could simply pick up where they'd left off before? Impossible.

"I shouldn't have let things get out of control. This wasn't why I brought you here."

"No. I'm sure it wasn't." She turned away, leaving him to pick up her coat he'd dropped on the floor, putting it away in the closet.

"Are you hungry?" he asked, when she made her way into his living room.

"Not really. And I don't need you to wait on me. I'm going to stretch out on the sofa to rest."

"Alyssa, don't." He quickened his pace so he could reach out to grab her arm. "Take my bed. I insist."

She tugged her arm away as if she couldn't tolerate his touch and crossed her arms over her chest. "I can't take your bed."

"Why not? I can't let you sleep on the sofa." He had two spare bedrooms, one he used as an office and the other just a junk room. When he'd invited her to move in with him, he'd intended to buy a bedroom set for the second bedroom. "Please, just this once, humor me."

She cocked a brow. "Just this once? I thought I'd been humoring you all along."

He couldn't disagree. "Maybe you have, but give me a break, will you? What if you tried to roll over on my sofa and fell to the floor, landing on your stomach? I'd never forgive myself."

Her mouth curved in a reluctant smile but then quickly faded. "Fine. I'll take your bed. But if you wake up with a sore back, don't blame me."

Better him having a sore back than her, but he didn't say anything. He headed down the hall and gestured to the bedroom, feeling somewhat awkward. "I'm, uh, sure you remember where everything is, right?"

Avoiding his gaze, she nodded. "Yes."

He tried not to remember the last time she'd been at his house, the night they'd made love several times, staying awake until dawn.

Pulling his gaze away from his bed, Jadon grabbed a pillow and a blanket from his linen closet. "Goodnight, Alyssa. Sleep well."

She didn't answer but closed his bedroom door with a loud click. He stared at it for a long moment before he turned and headed back into the living room to stretch out on his sofa.

The cloudy, snowy day should have made it easier for him to get some rest.

But even though he was dead tired, he couldn't sleep.

Images of Alyssa, in his bed, tortured him. He'd never made love to a pregnant woman before, but kissing Alyssa had been pure heaven. He found he was enthralled by the changes in her body, especially when he discovered she was still as responsive as ever. There must be something wrong with him to see Alyssa as more sexy than ever while soft and round, carrying his children.

From a medical perspective, he knew sexual intercourse wasn't dangerous during pregnancy. Alyssa had seemed to be as involved in their kiss as he'd been.

So why had he broken things off? Because sex didn't solve anything. They couldn't go back to being the carefree lovers they'd been. He didn't have a normal family, a normal future to offer her. He couldn't let himself fall for her. He had responsibilities. Obviously he'd help support her and the twins, but that was all he could do.

Knowing the truth didn't ease the ache in his groin. If he hadn't let his conscience get the better of him, they'd be sharing his bed right now.

He had no one to blame for his restlessness but himself.

CHAPTER SIX

ABOUT five hours later, Jadon woke up to the sound of his stomach growling. As he struggled upright on the not-so-comfortable-for-sleeping sofa, wincing against the light streaming through the living-room window, he wondered if Alyssa needed something to eat as well.

After all, she was eating for *three*. And working night shifts really messed up your body's normal rhythms. If he was hungry, she had to be starved.

Yawning widely, he shuffled down the hall toward the bathroom, pausing outside the closed door to his room and listening intently for any signs that she was up and awake. When after several moments he didn't hear a thing, he turned away. After spending a few minutes in the bathroom, he headed back to the kitchen.

Pursing his lips, he stared inside his fridge. Cooking wasn't exactly his strong suit, but he had eggs and milk. He opened a drawer and found cheese and a few green onions. He thought he still had some bacon bits, too. Just enough ingredients to scrape together an omelet. And some French toast if she wanted some.

He'd made both of the breakfasts for her before, he remembered, during those brief months of their steamy affair, and she'd seemed to enjoy them. So which one should he go with now?

Both, he decided. Couldn't go wrong with a choice.

He made a small pot of coffee, feeling a little guilty for drinking the brew in front of Alyssa but needing some caffeine to help clear his fuzzy, sleep-fogged brain.

He downed two cups of coffee, feeling more human afterward as he set about cracking eggs into a small bowl. He rather liked cooking for Alyssa.

Just as he finished preparing the meal, he heard the bathroom door close. Alyssa was awake, no doubt making one of her all-too-frequent trips to the bath-room.

He grabbed a rather beat-up metal TV tray left over from his college and medical school days, and loaded up the two plates he'd prepared. He added a tall glass of milk for Alyssa and then carried them out to the living room, just in time to catch her coming out of the bathroom.

She wore a pair of his old navy blue sweatpants and a sweatshirt, looking sleepily adorable despite the baggy clothes. He had to clench his teeth against a wave of desire.

"Alyssa? Are you hungry?" He hoped his voice didn't betray his lustful thoughts and he avoided her gaze by staring down at the food on the tray. "I have French toast and omelets."

She paused, and then nodded, showing no sign of her earlier ire. "You know, I am hungry. Thanks, it sounds great."

As she came closer, he noticed her face was pale and drawn, her earlier exhaustion still evident on her features.

Obviously, she needed a few more hours of sleep.

"Sit here on the sofa where it's more comfortable," he said, shoving aside the pillow and blanket he'd used. "Put your feet up and relax."

She walked slowly into the living room, gingerly sitting on one end of the sofa. She rested her feet on top of his coffee table with a muffled sigh.

He frowned in concern. "What's wrong?"

"I've been having some episodes of contractions," she admitted. "But they seem to be getting less frequent."

"Contractions?" His heart clenched and he stared helplessly at her rounded stomach. "Shouldn't you call Kim Rayborn?"

Alyssa bit her lip. "Yes," she agreed. "But I'd like to eat first. Last time this happened, they stopped on their own."

Last time? When? During the night? Or before she'd even gone to work?

Dammit, she had no business going back to work so soon.

He clenched his jaw and gently set the TV tray on her lap. Then he took the pillow off the sofa and tucked it beneath her ankles to protect them from the hard edge of the coffee table.

"Thanks," she murmured. She dug into the omelet and French toast meal he'd created with obvious enthusiasm. "Hmm. This is fantastic."

"I'm glad you like it." He sat beside her with his own plate, eating mechanically but not tasting a thing as he kept darting worried glances at Alyssa. When he realized his plate was clean yet he didn't remember tasting any of it, he set it aside with a grimace. "Alyssa, having contractions isn't good."

"It's not that bad. I've been timing them," she said defensively. "They're not regular and they don't last long."

He wanted to shake some sense into her. "You were on your feet the entire night—don't you think you might have overdone things just a bit?"

"Maybe," she said, avoiding his gaze.

He stifled a sigh. "Are you going to call Kim? She should be the final judge as to whether or not you should continue working."

Alyssa was silent for a long moment, before she finally looked at him. "I already called off work for tonight. I just don't think I can do another night shift like the one we had last night and I wanted to give them plenty of time to find someone to replace me."

"Thank heavens," he said, overwhelmed with relief. Finally she'd come to her senses. Now, if only he could convince her to stay here at his house where he could watch over her. "Your health, along with the babies', are your two main concerns. I'm sure they'll find someone to work your shift."

"I hope so." She frowned. "I don't like to leave them short-staffed. Look how busy we were being fully staffed."

"I know, but they're going to be working without you soon enough," he pointed out. "Especially if you deliver early. So pushing yourself isn't going to help."

She simply nodded as she ate the last bit of eggs and

toast on her plate. When she was finished, he stood and took the tray from her lap.

She frowned a little. "You cooked, so I should clean up."

Yeah, over his dead body she would. "Are you still having contractions?" he asked warily.

"Not in the last fifteen minutes," she said dryly. "Stop hovering, Jadon. The only thing Kim would tell me to do right now is go back on bed rest, which I can do on my own. I know my body well enough, and these few contractions aren't anything to worry about."

Maybe, but he didn't like it. He preferred having control of the situation, not waiting to see what might happen. He carried the dirty dishes back to the kitchen.

When he returned to the living room a few minutes later, she was lying back against the cushions with her eyes closed. He didn't want to disturb her but suddenly she opened her eyes.

"Jadon, this isn't going to work. You keep acting as if I'm going to fall apart. I think it's time you took me home."

"No." He stared at her for a long moment. "I'm happy to go to your apartment to pick up your things, but I'm not taking you home and leaving you alone."

Her eyes widened in surprise at his blunt response. "Excuse me?"

"You heard me. Don't ask me to do it, Alyssa, because I can't. Look at you! You're exhausted. You need to rest and you can't do that if you have to do everything for yourself." He rubbed the back of his neck, wishing he knew what to say to convince her. "Please. Stay here with me. At least until you deliver."

"Because you want to take care of me," she said, her tone laced with a hint of bitterness.

He didn't understand why that made her mad, but knew he had to step carefully. "No, it's not just that. I've missed you. And we have a lot to work through before the babies are born, don't you think?"

He sensed she liked that answer a little better, because she didn't immediately jump into another argument.

After what seemed like a lifetime, she slowly nodded. "All right, Jadon. I'll stay for a short time." His relief must have been obvious, because she hastily added, "But only if you bring my bedroom set here so that we both have a place to sleep. I refuse to kick you out of your bed."

Logically, he knew sharing his bed with her was out of the question. Still, that common-sense thought didn't stop his body from reacting at the possibility.

This move was for Alyssa and the twins, not for him.

"It's a deal," he said quickly, before she could change her mind.

Alyssa had truckloads of doubts regarding the wisdom of her decision to stay with Jadon, especially the way he sprung into action, calling Simon Carter for help and making a list of everything he needed to bring over from her apartment. He left so quickly when Simon arrived to pick him up she didn't have time to voice her concerns.

He'd said he'd missed her. And unfortunately he was right when he'd said they had a lot of details to work through before the twins were born. No matter how much she wanted to remain independent, she couldn't be foolish about it. And despite how she'd reassured him, the contractions worried her. What if she couldn't work anymore? She didn't want to end up like her mother, obsessed with making ends meet. Hadn't that been the real reason she'd insisted on going back to work so soon?

And now look at her. She'd overdone it, big-time. With slow, deep breaths she performed the relaxation techniques she'd learned in Lamaze class. The contractions came and went, but were much less now that she was resting quietly.

She'd missed her last session thanks to her hospitalization. It wasn't that big a deal, the last class being to watch a video of a birth, and she'd seen one during her nurse's training. Kylie, too, had not only had Ben but as a paramedic had also seen a birth. Kylie would be a great birthing coach.

Would Jadon mind knowing Kylie was her birthing coach? Maybe, although it wasn't as if he'd been around to attend classes with her. She remembered Megan, the birthing instructor, telling them there was a DVD version of the class available, too. Jadon would probably be more than willing to watch it.

Wait a minute, was she seriously thinking of asking Jadon to be her birthing coach?

Yes. She was.

She closed her eyes with a weary sigh. Moving in with him was definitely a mistake. They were soon-to-be parents without the benefit of a loving relationship. And she was beginning to care about him, too much. And what did he want from her? Nothing. He'd been the one to break off their kiss. He'd been clear about how much he wanted her to stay here with him, but only because she needed help. Not because he was interested in pursuing an intimate relationship. That much was obvious.

Her cheeks flushed and her breath shortened as she relived the kiss. For some strange reason—maybe an excess of hormones—she was burning with pent-up sexual frustration. She'd never realized how easy it was to get sexually stimulated while pregnant.

She'd wanted Jadon.

Had practically thrown herself at him.

Only to be turned down.

She opened her eyes and gazed morosely at her large belly. Of course Jadon hadn't been interested, why would he? She was the size of a house!

Before she could wallow too deep in her pool of self-pity, Jadon and Simon returned with the first load of stuff from her apartment. Jadon hauled in the mattress from outside, laughing and shaking snowflakes off his dark hair as he entered the house. She couldn't tear her gaze away from him, especially the way his muscles flexed as he maneuvered the mattress down the hallway to the spare bedroom he'd already cleared out for her.

So far, Jadon certainly didn't look as if he minded the extra work. Or that he was regretting asking her to stay. Did he really want to talk about the possibility of a future? And could she trust him if he did? How could she know if Jadon would really stick around for the long haul? Especially with the stress of raising not just one baby but two?

"Hi, Alyssa," Simon greeted her, coming in behind Jadon, lugging a large suitcase she hoped was full of her maternity clothes. She felt like a lost waif in Jadon's sweats. "How are you and the babies feeling?"

"We're fine," she said with a smile. Simon was a nice guy—in fact, they'd gone out on a couple of dates prior to her meeting Jadon, but there just hadn't been any spark. She was glad they'd been able to remain friends. "Thanks for moving all my stuff."

"No problem. I think it's very good that you're staying here with Jadon," Simon said in a serious tone. "You shouldn't be alone, not with all the complications you've had."

"I only had complications because I was silly enough to fall into Lake Michigan," she protested. "Not because of my pregnancy in general."

"It wasn't silly to save Ben's life," Jadon said, walking back through the living room.

"No, but I should have been able to get Ben out of the water without falling in." She wrinkled her nose. "I didn't factor in how much larger and lower my center of gravity is."

"All that matters is that you're both safe," Simon said.

"Come on, Simon." Jadon clapped him on the shoulder. "Help me carry her bed frame inside."

"How did you get all this stuff over here?" Alyssa asked with a puzzled frown.

"Jadon rented a truck," Simon answered over his shoulder. "And a good thing because the four-wheel drive sure helped us get up that hill on your street."

She vaguely remembered Jadon saying something

about the slippery, snow-covered hill on the street leading to her apartment. It was one of the reasons she'd ended up here with him in the first place. She didn't ask any more questions until they had everything moved in.

Including her small, lopsided Christmas tree.

"I can't believe you brought it along," she murmured as Jadon set it up in the corner of the living room, directly in her line of vision from her position on the sofa. Simon had left a few minutes previously, to return the rented truck.

He rocked back on his heels, flashing her a quizzical, sideways glance. "Well, I couldn't just leave it there in your apartment, the poor thing looked lonely enough as it was. And since I didn't have any Christmas decorations up of my own, I figured this would cheer you up better than nothing."

"Thanks, Jadon." She was foolishly touched by his consideration. "I've been really looking forward to Christmas this year."

"Yeah?" His smile was infectious.

"Yeah. So, uh, do you have to work tonight?"

"No, I'm off the next two nights." He spent more time making adjustments to the tree, until he finally stood and put his hands on his hips in disgust. "I swear I've done everything to straighten this tree. Nothing works. It's still crooked."

Her lips twitched at his vexed tone. She lifted her shoulder in a shrug. "I kind of like it that way."

He rolled his eyes. "Figures. Okay, I give up, then. The tree is up, and Simon helped me put your bed back together, so all we need to do is unpack your clothes. Do you want me to do that for you?"

"Ah, no," she said hastily. It was bad enough that her maternity clothes probably looked like giant tents, she didn't need him going through stuff any more than he already had. "I can do it."

"But you're supposed to be resting."

She took her feet off the table and struggled to her feet. "I've been doing nothing but resting." And despite the fact she'd already been up to the bathroom several times, she needed to go again. She paused long enough to put a hand on Jadon's arm. "Thanks, Jadon. I mean it. I appreciate how you went out of your way to bring everything over here."

"Hey, having you move in was my idea, remember?" he joked. But he placed his hand over hers, squeezing it gently. "Everything will be fine."

She wished, really wished that were true. If only he'd see her as a woman, and not as a burden to care for.

Jadon couldn't sleep. Across the hall he could hear Alyssa's bed frame creaking as she tossed and turned, and figured she wasn't getting much rest either. For long moments he stared at the ceiling, fighting the urge to check on her. She'd claimed he was hovering too much, and he supposed she was right.

He couldn't help it. The very idea of Alyssa delivering the twins early sent him into panic mode.

She'd be fine. The twins would be fine. He couldn't control her labor. He had to lighten up a bit.

He jerked upright when Alyssa cried out. In alarm, he leaped out of bed and dashed into her room.

She was moaning, thrashing in the covers, obviously caught in the throes of a bad dream.

"Alyssa," he whispered, putting a calming hand on her shoulder. "Wake up. It's only a dream."

He had to repeat himself several times before his low voice penetrated her subconscious.

"What?" She blinked at him through the darkness. "Jadon?"

"I think you were having a bad dream," he told her, sitting on the edge of her bed, wearing only his boxers. "Are you okay?"

She stared at him for several heartbeats and then slowly nodded. "It was a bad dream. Some guy was chasing me and being pregnant I couldn't run fast enough to get away from him. For some reason he wanted to hurt my babies. When he grabbed me I thought I was going to die. Sorry if I woke you."

"You didn't wake me. I wasn't sleeping." He was glad he'd come in. What an awful dream. "Do you want me to get you something?"

"No." She pushed up and propped herself on her elbows. "But now that I'm awake I need to go to the bathroom."

He chuckled and held out his hand. She took his hand, using his strength to lever herself out of bed.

"Thanks," she murmured, moving past him. Her hair brushed against his bare chest, leaving tiny shocks of awareness.

Jadon took a deep breath and rubbed the back of his neck, knowing he should go back to his own room. Alyssa was fine. He wasn't needed here anymore.

But he waited until she returned. Her white nightgown left her sexy shoulders bare and he had to swallow hard not to show his reaction. "Are you sure you're okay?"

"Yes." Her nightgown rose a bit as she swung her legs back into bed. "The dream was far too real, though."

He didn't want to leave, but forced himself to move toward the door. "Call me if you need me."

"I will. Uh, Jadon?"

He swung back toward her. "Yes?"

"You don't think my dream is some sort of a premonition of something bad happening to the babies, do you?"

"No, of course not." He came back and sat next to her.

She shivered. "It was just so real."

"Do you want me to stay with you for a while?" He didn't want to leave her like this. "I'll hold you until you can fall asleep."

She must have been more shaken than he'd thought because she nodded. "Maybe, just a few minutes, if you don't mind."

All of his senses went on red alert. Lying beside her didn't sound like much, but he was already half-aroused; he wasn't sure he could trust himself to be so close to her.

But his thoughts didn't make it to his mouth. "Sure," he heard himself say. "I don't mind."

"I'm sorry to be such a problem," Alyssa said as he slid beneath the covers on the opposite side of the bed. She lay on her side, facing away from him.

"You're not," he promised, gently snuggling up behind her. He slid his arm under her pillow so he could hold her closer.

"That feels good," she murmured on a sigh, relaxing

against him. "It's hard to get comfortable. My back aches constantly."

With her bottom pressed firmly against his groin he could relate, since he was anything but comfortable. Yet he wasn't about to complain.

Not even when she slipped into sleep, leaving him rock-hard and wide-awake.

CHAPTER SEVEN

ALYSSA woke up with the vague sensation of being nestled in a cocoon. Safe and warm. A sleepy smile curved her mouth. Jadon had stayed with her all night and the nightmare hadn't returned.

How sweet was that?

She enjoyed listening to Jadon's deep, even breaths as he slept beside her. Soon, though, she became aware of his body pressed against her. And she grew warm. Extremely warm. Hot. Very hot.

Aroused.

During the night, the lower edge of her nightgown had crept up around her waist. Jadon's erection pressed urgently against her bottom and his hand rested dangerously close to her breast.

Her breasts, especially her nipples, were hypersensitive. When his hand moved, cupping her breast, she sucked in a quick breath. His fingers lightly brushed the tip of her nipple and instantly her body grew ready. Her breath came in short gasps as she became fully awake. Moisture gathered deep between her thighs and she instinctively arched against him, pressing her bottom more fully against the hard ridge of his desire, wanting him to touch her. Everywhere.

Maybe the reason she yearned for this intimacy with Jadon was because she was pregnant and hadn't felt very attractive these past few months. Despite the twins growing in her abdomen, she was more than a mother-to-be.

She was a woman. And she hadn't been with a man in months. Since the last time she'd been with Jadon.

Obviously meeting men when you were pregnant wasn't easy, but it wouldn't have mattered anyway because she hadn't wanted any other man but Jadon. How could she have convinced herself it was nothing more than an affair?

He groaned, a low raspy sound near her ear as he caressed her breast again. She couldn't see his face to know if he was awake. Or still half-asleep.

She wasn't sure she cared, except for the possibility that if he woke up and realized what he was doing, he might pull away again, like he had after their kiss. And if he did that, she'd probably scream with frustration.

His knee pressed between her legs and she eagerly parted her thighs, opening herself to him. His hand left her breast, lightly caressed her round belly and then moved lower still, until he reached the juncture of her thighs. She held her breath with anticipation as he moved her silky panties out of the way and touched her where she needed him the most.

With his fingers caressing her from the front and his hard erection behind her, Alyssa was trapped in pleasure and didn't want to move. Yet at the same time she ached with the need to have him inside her.

"Please," she whispered, subtly lifting her hips to press against him again.

"Are you sure?" he murmured near her ear, before trailing a string of heated kisses along the side of her neck.

Was he kidding? He was finally treating her like a woman he was attracted to and he thought she had doubts?

"Yes. I'm sure." She pressed urgently against him.

"Easy now," he said, kissing her again and gently stroking her cleft, sending shock waves of pleasure through her body. "Relax. Let me do all the work."

Fine with her if he wanted to do all the work, but could he get on with it? Relaxing when you were aroused was impossible. And he was treating her like she was fragile spun glass instead of a woman who knew exactly what she wanted. She didn't want him to hold back. Reaching around, she tried to pull him closer. She was more than ready. Like ready right now.

He brought her close to the edge of an orgasm before he managed to get rid of her panties and push his boxers out of the way. Her body offered no resistance as he slid deep. The feeling of his thickness inside her, skin against skin, without the barrier of protection, was exquisite.

"Yes. Finally," she gasped.

He pressed another kiss below her ear and pulled her over so that she was lying more fully on top of him. This position not only gave him more access to thrust inside her but also freed up his other hand to caress her breasts.

The sensation was dizzying.

"Jadon," she moaned, wanting the pleasure to last forever yet striving for more.

"Alyssa, tell me if I hurt you," he said between careful thrusts.

"You're not." He was holding back again and that wasn't what she wanted. Then his fingers found the super-sensitive spot between her legs and she gasped, arching her back.

Her climax hit hard and she cried out with pleasure as Jadon crested his pinnacle seconds later. For long moments, the only audible sound in the room was their heavy breathing.

Jadon slid her over to the side, yet held her close. She was happy they'd made love but wished Jadon could have let himself go, the way he once had.

"Alyssa, are you all right? I didn't hurt you or the babies, did I?"

Exasperated, she swiveled her head around to look at him. "Why would you have hurt me? Do you think I'm the only pregnant woman in the world to have sex?"

He propped his head up on his elbow, gazing down at her, a frown puckering his brow. "No, but you were having contractions yesterday. I should have used more restraint."

His gaze was so serious, she knew he was really bothered by the idea that he might have caused some harm. Yet he acted as if he wished they hadn't made love. "Are you always going to treat me like I'm fragile?"

He was taken aback by her sharp tone. "You almost died. Every time I think of you delivering the babies early, my gut gets tied up in knots."

Surprised by his revelation, she arched a brow. Jadon didn't talk about his feelings, ever. "I'm fine. I wish things could go back to the way they were before."

"You can't go back. You're a mother now."

So she wasn't a woman? "And you're a father."

"I know." His expression turned grim. "That wasn't exactly part of my plan."

She tried not to take offense at his honesty. "Is that the real reason you left?"

"No." Jadon pulled away, reaching for his boxers. Apparently his brief display of emotion was over. "I didn't know you were pregnant."

"Would it have mattered?"

He paused, before continuing to pull his boxers on. "Of course it would have mattered. I would have stayed in touch with you while I was gone."

He still would have left. Even now, he was putting distance between them. They'd made love, but nothing had really changed. He was still holding her at arm's length, keeping himself emotionally apart.

And she wasn't satisfied with that. Not anymore.

"Why don't you take a shower? I'll make breakfast."

"Don't wait on me." She didn't hide her annoyance. "I'm perfectly capable of making my own breakfast."

He hardly glanced at her when she slid from the bed to find her clothes. "I'm cooking anyway, so it's no bother."

He had an answer for everything. Discouraged, Alyssa showered, using the hot water to wash away her disappointment. Afterward, she pulled out the first maternity outfit she found. It didn't matter what she wore. Jadon wouldn't notice anyway.

Stop it, she admonished herself. So maybe she and Jadon weren't a happy couple. Too bad. He was the father of her babies and she just had to find a way to deal with it.

She walked to the kitchen, where Jadon had made steamy bowls of oatmeal, topped with cinnamon, brown sugar and raisins. As she sat down, a contraction tightened her abdomen.

Hard.

Worse than she'd experienced the day before.

She mentally ticked off the seconds until the contraction eased, noting that it lasted for over a minute.

Hmm. Not good. She continued eating her breakfast without saying anything to Jadon. He'd only start worrying again. And she wasn't in the mood to be coddled.

But clearly she'd have to give Kim a call. Maybe she'd be lucky and the contractions would stop.

Jadon watched Alyssa eating her oatmeal and mentally talked himself out of taking her back to bed for an encore.

Did she have any idea how much he wanted her? She looked so beautiful, with her dark hair falling in waves around her shoulders, the bright pink long-sleeved maternity top emphasizing the plumpness of her breasts and her gently curved stomach.

Just looking at her made him sweat. He shouldn't have stayed the night in her bed, but he couldn't find the energy for regrets. Not when their morning had started off so great.

He'd been half-asleep that morning when she'd moved against him, silently urging him to touch her. At some level he'd known exactly what he was doing, yet he hadn't been able to make himself stop.

Especially when Alyssa had clearly been egging him on.

But then they'd argued and the time of closeness had

gone. He didn't understand what she wanted from him. No, he hadn't planned on being a father, but he was here with her now, wasn't he? Didn't that count for something?

They couldn't go back. They had to figure out how to move forward. And no matter what, he couldn't give her the happy, close-knit family she wanted. His fault, not hers.

Alyssa rose from her seat at the table, moving stiffly. "Are you all right?" he asked, sure he had hurt her.

She rolled her eyes. "I'm going to sit on the sofa. Do you mind?"

"Not at all." He needed to clean up the kitchen and take a shower, too. "What do you want to do today? Christmas shopping?"

Her annoyance faded and her eyes brightened. "Yes. I'd like to pick up something for Kylie and Seth, and a special present for Ben."

"Good. Let me clean up and shower first."

On his way to the bathroom he heard his cell phone ringing. So he turned back, searching through his pile of dirty laundry, another task he'd have to tackle soon, for the device.

His mother's number was on the display screen. Dread squeezed his intestines and twisted, hard. God, no. Not again. Wishing he could ignore the call, he slowly opened the phone and lifted it to his ear. "Hi, Mom. What is it? What's wrong?"

"Nothing," she swiftly reassured him. "How are you?"

He frowned, not understanding. "Nothing is wrong? You're sure? Jack is doing okay?"

"Yes, actually Jack seems to be doing better. This

new doctor has started a whole new medication regimen and so far Jack is going along with it. He likes the new doctor anyway."

The new doctor he'd pulled strings for his brother to see was a female, which might explain why Jack liked her but he didn't care since Dr. Elizabeth Cranberg was also a renowned expert in treating patients like Jack.

"Good. I'm glad." He knew Jack probably had a long way to go but maybe this was a turning point for his brother. Maybe there was a chance for Jack to lead a relatively normal life.

Foolish hope swelled in his chest. Maybe someday he'd have a normal life, too. "Will you keep me informed on how things go?"

"Of course." His mother didn't sound tired and exhausted like she had before. Instead, it seemed like things were cautiously optimistic with Jack. "Anyway, I called because I'd like to make some plans for the holiday. Do you know when you might be coming home to visit?"

Oh, boy, he'd forgotten his mother's request to have the whole family together for Christmas. Including his father, whom he hadn't seen in years. The stress of Jack's problems had ruined his parents' marriage and his father's subsequent second marriage, too. He needed to tell his parents about Alyssa and the babies, but if he did that, they'd expect her to come along.

He sank down on the edge of his bed, trying to figure out the best way to handle things. He didn't want Alyssa exposed to his problems. She hadn't signed on to be Jack's caretaker, that was his role. He didn't want her involved.

"I have to work Christmas," he reminded her. "I'll see if I can get a couple of consecutive days off, all right?"

"Okay." He could hear the disappointment in his mother's voice. "Are you sure you can't get off for Christmas?"

"I was off work for over four months," he reminded her. "At this point, I'm not in a position to ask for favors."

"I understand," she said hastily, knowing very well why he'd needed to take that time off in the first place. Things had been bad. Jack had gotten completely out of control. "We can celebrate whichever days work best for you."

"All right, I'll be in touch."

"Bye, Jadon. I love you."

Guilt swelled his throat. "I love you, too, Mom."

After he hung up the phone, Jadon realized he couldn't keep the truth about his twin brother a secret from Alyssa for much longer. Alyssa needed to know about Jack, so she'd understand when he had to leave again. And why he couldn't give her what she needed. What she deserved.

He needed to explain everything.

From the very beginning.

Alyssa sat on the sofa, taking slow, deep breaths while waiting for Kim to return her call. She hoped Kim would call while Jadon was still in the shower, but already she could hear him leaving the bathroom and making his way to his bedroom.

The contractions hadn't eased very much. They hadn't gotten any worse, but they certainly hadn't gotten any better either.

She nibbled on her lower lip, wondering what to do. She didn't want to rush to the hospital, yet the medication to prevent contractions didn't seem to be working very well either.

If she didn't hear from Kim in a few hours, she'd go in. Better to be safe than sorry.

"So, have you thought about where you'd like to go Christmas shopping?" Jadon asked, striding into the living room.

"Uh, actually, I'm feeling a bit tired. Do you think it's okay if we do a little online shopping instead of going out?"

His eyebrows rose in surprise. "We can, but are you sure? I thought you'd be ready for a change in scenery." He glanced toward the window. "It's not snowing."

"It's not the weather. I've had a couple of contractions," she admitted, knowing he was going to ask in a minute anyway. "And, yes, I've already called Kim Rayborn but she's busy with a delivery so I left a message for her to call me back."

"Dammit," Jadon muttered. "We shouldn't have made love."

"You don't know for sure sex caused the contractions." She removed her feet from the top of the coffee table and struggled to stand.

"Where are you going?" Jadon asked in alarm, jumping over to her. His strong hands lifted her from the soft sofa cushions without difficulty. "Stay put. I'll get my laptop computer if you want to shop online."

She sighed. "I'm going to the bathroom. You can't help me with that."

"Oh. Okay." His expression was sheepish. "I'll turn on the computer while you're gone."

"All right." She took a few steps but then stopped as

another contraction hit. Moisture gushed down between her thighs and for a horrified moment she thought she'd lost control of her bladder. But looking down, she realized there was a lot of fluid. Clear fluid. Amniotic fluid.

"Um, Jadon? You'd better forget about the computer. I think my waters just broke."

CHAPTER EIGHT

ALYSSA tried not to show her panic as one of her ED coworkers, Susan, wheeled her upstairs to the third-floor labor and delivery area.

Kim crossed over to greet her as she rolled in. "Alyssa, how are you? I just picked up your message and suddenly you're here. What happened? Have your contractions gotten worse?"

"My waters broke." She kept a hand on her stomach, forcing a smile for Jadon's sake. "And yes, the contractions have gotten worse. Not only are they coming more frequently and regularly at seven minutes apart, but they're lasting longer, too."

"Well, it's clear those twins are not going to wait any longer to be born," Kim said. "Looks like we'll be getting you ready for delivery."

"They're still pretty early, aren't they?" Jadon asked, concern evident in his tone.

Kim nodded. "A bit. But they're thirty-one weeks along now, which is one more week's worth of growing. I'm sure everything will be just fine."

A week's worth of growing didn't sound like very much. And she wished more than anything she could believe everything would be fine. Reality set in as another contraction tightened her abdomen.

"Neenah?" A nurse hurried over when Kim called, a young woman Alyssa didn't recognize. "Let's get Alyssa settled into room six. I'd like to get her twins hooked up to the fetal monitors to see how they're doing."

"Of course," Neenah said, taking over behind the wheelchair. "Alyssa? My name is Neenah Burnes and I'll be your nurse for today."

Alyssa nodded, but her mind was struggling to come to grips with what was happening. She was in labor. She was going to deliver her babies. Twins. Jiminy Cricket, how on earth was she going to manage? What if she couldn't handle the pressure of raising a baby? Two babies? Her mother had struggled with the demands of single parenthood.

At least Jadon was here, so she wasn't nearly as alone as her mother had been. And even though she wanted more from him at the moment, she'd take what she could get.

Neenah helped her move from the wheelchair onto the bed, shooing Jadon out so she could change into a hospital gown. He'd been suspiciously quiet and Alyssa couldn't help wondering if he regretted being here with her. She suspected the prospect of fatherhood scared him.

Would he stay with her during the delivery? Or should she call Kylie to be her coach?

When she was settled in bed, the fetal heart monitors in place, she took several deep breaths, trying to relax.

Stress was not good. Especially not now.

"Jadon?" she called.

"I'm here." He came in, and took her hand in his. They'd given him scrubs to wear. "What's wrong? Another contraction?"

"Yes." They were coming even more frequently now. "Kylie was supposed to be my labor coach. But I'd rather have you. If you don't mind."

He stared at her for a long moment. "I don't mind. They're my babies, too."

"I know." She sucked in a harsh breath as the contraction crested, sending shock waves of pain through her whole body. "Oh, boy, that was a strong one," she whispered as it finally eased.

Jadon cradled her hand in both of his. "It's okay, Alyssa. I'm here. I'll help you through this."

He wasn't going to leave, or call Kylie. He was going to stay.

"I need to do a quick exam, to see how far along you are," Kim said, coming into the room dressed in fresh scrubs and pulling on a pair of gloves.

Alyssa couldn't help it, she tightened her grip on Jadon's hand, full of apprehensive fear. He pulled up a chair with his foot and sat right next to her bed, staying close.

Kim lifted the sheet and Alyssa's hospital gown and then gently eased her thighs open. "Good heavens, you're already five centimeters dilated. I suspect these babies are going to be born very quickly."

"Good." Another contraction tightened her abdomen and she glanced over at Jadon. "Don't leave me," she begged through clenched teeth.

Not just for now, but forever. She didn't want Jadon to leave her alone ever again, but as the contraction grew tighter and tighter, she didn't have a chance to explain.

"I won't," Jadon promised.

She wanted nothing more than to believe him.

Watching Alyssa suffer through one contraction after another was enough to make him swear off sex forever. Sweat beaded on his forehead, trickling in rivulets down his back, and he wasn't even the one doing all the work.

This was all his fault, for not having enough self-control to protect her from becoming pregnant in the first place all those months ago. And, again, for allowing his desire to overcome his common sense that morning.

He was about to become a father.

Panic tightened his throat. Juggling his responsibilities with Jack had been hard enough before, but the twins' impending birth just made it that much more complicated.

He'd promised Alyssa he'd stay, and he'd sensed she meant more than just during the delivery. But what if Jack needed him again? He couldn't abandon his mother. If Jack needed him, he'd be forced to leave.

He turned his attention to Alyssa, and within moments the entire labor room had been converted into a delivery suite, complete with a neonatal team on standby in case the twins needed them.

He was a doctor, had seen births a couple of times before, but nothing could have prepared him for the miracle of watching his children being born.

"Come on, Alyssa, one more big push," Kim was saying. "You're almost there. The first baby is crowning."

Tears streaked Alyssa's cheeks but she didn't sob or cry out. She simply gritted her teeth and pushed, nearly crushing all the bones in his hand in the process.

"Wonderful! Perfect. Congratulations, you have a beautiful daughter."

Jadon's grin almost split his face. "Can you see her, Lys? She's absolutely beautiful."

Alyssa nodded. "Is she okay? How big do you think she is?"

"We'll get her weighed and measured in a jiffy," Kim promised, handing the infant over to Renee, one of the neonatal ICU nurses who was part of the resuscitation team. She took the baby to the first isolette and began the exam with the help of the neonatologist.

Jadon knew they needed to do an Apgar assessment on the baby, along with placing the proper identification bracelets, so he didn't leave Alyssa's side, even though he was anxious to meet his daughter.

He was a father. He could barely wrap his mind around the concept. More responsibility. Double the responsibility.

"Oh, no, another contraction," Alyssa whimpered.

"This might be the placenta," Kim warned. "I know it's tough, Alyssa, but hang in there. You're halfway there."

"Only halfway," she groaned, panting through another contraction. "Doesn't seem fair."

Jadon leaned down to press his lips to her forehead. He shared her pain. "I know. I wish I could do this for you."

"You and me both," she said with a groan.

"Knight baby girl number one weighs in at three

pounds, nine ounces," Renee announced for everyone to hear. "And she's seventeen and a half inches long."

Alyssa smiled. "Three pounds nine ounces is pretty good, right? Is she breathing on her own?"

"Yes, so far she's breathing fine. Don't worry," Kim told her. "Your job is to deliver this next baby."

As if on cue, another contraction caused her to grab Jadon's hand again. Her determined gaze met his. "I think baby number two is on his or her way."

Jadon wasn't sure what to expect. He was an identical twin, but women Alyssa's age were prone to fraternal twins. Either way, he didn't care. He was still in awe about having a daughter. "Slow, easy breaths," he instructed. "Don't think about the pain, think about the baby."

The second birth went faster and within another minute Alyssa was pushing again.

"Congrats, you have another beautiful daughter," Kim announced with a laugh. "Beautiful twin girls."

The second baby girl was passed on to the neonatal team as well and from where he stood, Jadon could tell the second baby was slightly smaller than the first one. They didn't look identical, but they were pretty small so it was difficult to tell. Although a little more than three and a half pounds was not a bad size for a preemie.

And if both babies could breathe without any help from a mask or a ventilator, that was a minor miracle in itself.

"You did a great job," Jadon said, kissing Alyssa lightly on the mouth. "I'm proud of you."

"Thanks." This time she smiled through her tears. "I can't believe we have daughters."

"Beautiful twin daughters," Kim corrected with a smile. "Have you thought of names yet?"

Alyssa nodded. "I've chosen Grace Aubrey for the older baby and Gretchen Louise for the younger one." Her gaze darted to his. "I, uh, hope you don't mind."

What could he say? It wasn't as if they'd been together these past few months, planning for this day. Alyssa had been on her own. Of course she'd picked names for the babies.

"Grace and Gretchen are beautiful names." A part of him wished their last names would be listed as his, rather than Alyssa's last name of Knight, but that wasn't meant to be.

"My grandmother's name was Grace and my mom's name was Louise, so I wanted to include both their names in their memory if the babies were girls," she explained, as if expecting some sort of argument.

"Alyssa, the names are fine," he reassured her. "I love them, don't worry."

She nodded and relaxed. "When can we hold them?" she asked Kim. "I'm anxious to see my babies."

"Just a few more minutes and the neonatal team should be finished with them." Kim began cleaning up the delivery area. "One good thing about having small babies is that you didn't need an episiotomy and there are no vaginal tears either. You should heal up very nicely."

"One bright spot as I'm trying to breast-feed two babies," Alyssa said with a dry laugh. But then she caught the doctor's hand, giving it a grateful squeeze. "Thanks, Kim. For everything."

"My pleasure." Kim glanced at Jadon, including him as well. "Congrats to both of you."

"Knight baby girl number two is three pounds, three

ounces, and is seventeen and a quarter inches long," Renee announced. "She's breathing on her own, too."

Three-three wasn't bad at all. Jadon grinned as the tight knot in his stomach relaxed a bit. "Gretchen Louise. The younger, smaller baby is Gretchen."

"And the older one is Grace Aubrey," Alyssa chimed in. "Can we hold them now?"

"You sure can. Here's Grace for you, Mom. And Gretchen for you, Dad." Renee and another nurse handed each of them a tightly wrapped pink bundle. "We don't want to keep them out of the isolettes too long. We still need to keep a close eye on them, but bonding is important, too."

Jadon gazed at Gretchen's small, perfect face, her tiny lips, her button nose and her tiny, tiny eyelashes with an overwhelming sense of awe.

He glanced at Alyssa and in that moment they shared a special intimacy, a bond that shook him to the soles of his feet.

Together, they'd created these baby girls.

Looking at Alyssa holding Grace and the way Gretchen slept so peacefully in his arms, he realized what he'd told her earlier was true. There was no turning back. He was a father now.

This new, precious family was a part of his future. His and Alyssa's future.

If only he knew how in the world he was going to make it work.

Alyssa rested for a few hours after the birth as the process had totally worn her out, but when she awoke she was alone in her room. She missed her babies. On the bedside table were two photographs, so she picked them up to gaze at the small pictures of Grace and Gretchen that the neonatal resuscitation team had given her.

The babies were small, but doing amazingly well. Kim had explained that the stress of her labor over the past few days had helped the babies develop enough surfactant in their lungs to enable them to breathe on their own.

At least, so far they were breathing on their own. The girls might need some help from a CPAP machine, which wasn't as invasive as a breathing tube and ventilator, if they didn't maintain regular breathing patterns, keeping an acceptable level of oxygen in the blood.

Renee had explained the concerns about intermittent apnea, a common phenomenon with preemies. They could breathe on their own, but it was almost as if they exerted so much energy to do the work they got tired out and stopped breathing for a few seconds.

So the baby girls would need to be on the heart and apnea monitors for a while, not to mention kept warm since their tiny brains weren't fully developed yet to keep their temperatures stable. Hence the pictures, since Alyssa couldn't have the babies housed in her room.

She was relieved they were doing so well.

Yet she didn't want to look at pictures, she wanted to hold her daughters, touch them. Cuddle them.

Was Jadon in the neonatal nursery with them now? She was fairly certain he was. She bit her lip, anxiety creeping back into her chest. He'd been so wonderful through all this, taken on the role of being her birthing coach without making her feel guilty.

Her baby girls were seven weeks early. What would

she do once they were big enough to come home? She knew she shouldn't just plan on going back to Jadon's house but if she didn't, how would she manage to nurse them both while still managing to get some rest?

Was Jadon's invitation to stay with him still open? She didn't want her babies to suffer in any way. What if after a few weeks of no sleep he changed his mind?

Stop looking for trouble, she warned herself. Take it slowly, one day at a time, and the future would sort itself out when it was ready.

Sage advice. Now, if only she could heed it.

She swung her legs out of the bed and stood, feeling only a slight twinge of discomfort after her delivery. Reaching for a robe, she put it on, then walked out into the hallway to get directions to the neonatal intensive care unit.

"Right here," Amanda, a helpful nurse, informed her. "We actually don't call them neonatal ICUs any more, we call it a level-three nursery. But it's right next to the level-two and level-one nurseries. As your babies progress, they'll move down to the less acute area."

"Good to know," Alyssa admitted. Neonatal was not her area of expertise.

In the level-three nursery, most of the babies lying in their isolettes looked extremely tiny. She was somewhat relieved to realize her daughters were the largest babies in the group.

She stood in front of their isolettes, surprised to note Jadon wasn't there. One nurse approached with a warm smile.

"Hi, my name is Carla. I'm the second-shift nurse taking care of Grace and Gretchen."

"Hello, I'm Alyssa, the proud mother of these two. Oh, look, Gretch is waking up," she said, leaning over when Gretchen began to stir.

"She is waking up. It's about time as she's been sleeping quite a bit. What a wonderful early Christmas present you have, hmm?"

Alyssa smiled weakly. "A better Christmas present would be to have them home with me."

"True, but if they grow nicely and don't run into trouble, that is a distinct possibility. Now, would you like to hold them? Both at once or one at a time?"

"Maybe just Gretchen, since she's awake." Alyssa figured she'd need to learn how to manage both babies at the same time eventually, but for now she thought easing into the process of learning about her daughters might be the better approach.

"Okay. Both girls have apnea monitors on, so we can watch their heart rates and breathing. I'll fetch a warm blanket." Carla hurried off, returning with a warm fuzzy pink blanket.

She opened the isolette and competently lifted Gretchen with one hand, taking care not to disturb the wires connecting the patches to the infant's chest or the tiny IV as she slid the warm blanket underneath with the other hand. After tucking her cozily inside, she gently lifted Gretchen out and set the bundle in the crook of Alyssa's arm. "Here you go."

"Oh, she's so adorable." And tiny, especially being the smaller of the two. She clutched the baby protectively to her chest, infused with a wave of love. She'd do anything for her children. Anything.

Gretchen moved her head toward her breast in a

rooting movement, her tiny mouth making sucking motions. Alyssa drew a quick breath of excitement and glanced at Carla. "Look, do you think she'll be able to nurse?"

"It's possible," Carla agreed with a smile. "Your milk hasn't come in, but the colostrum they'll receive is even more healthy than milk. And worth a try, don't you think?"

"Yes." She was a little uncertain how to go about the whole process but Carla was great, helping her with techniques to encourage Gretchen to latch on. The baby only suckled for a few minutes before stopping.

"Don't worry, preemie babies do tire easily. Once your milk comes in more fully, we'll give intermittent feedings of your breast milk as often as the babies need it."

"But what if they're not strong enough to drink as much as they need?" Alyssa asked.

"We'll give feedings through a nasogastric tube."

A nasogastric tube didn't sound good, but she tried not to show her discouragement. Carla tucked Gretchen back in her isolette and then drew Grace out for her turn. Gracie latched on to her nipple a little quicker than Gretchen, but also seemed to get tired quickly. Alyssa wasn't sure either of the babies got any nourishment at all from the attempt.

"How am I going to keep up with breast-feeding both of them?" she asked, after she'd finished with Grace. The responsibility was daunting and she suddenly doubted her ability to be a good mother to the twins. "At this rate, they might need to be fed every hour."

Carla put a reassuring hand on her shoulder. "Nursing is a wonderful experience, but the nutritional value of your breast milk is what's most important for these little ones. Even if they can't nurse for lengthy periods, they can get the nourishment they need if you pump your breasts and freeze your milk. We can feed them through a nasogastric tube if need be and then through a bottle. At least with bottle feedings, Dad can be more involved, too."

Jadon. The image of his strong, large hands holding and feeding their daughters filled her with a mixture of longing and trepidation. Would he stick around for the long term? Or would he get tired of the responsibility of having a family and leave, like her father had?

At least now he could stop being so protective of her. Although she suspected he'd shower the babies with his concern instead.

"Was Jadon here?" she asked Carla.

"Yes, he spent a lot of time with the girls. He asked Dr. Downer, the neonatologist, lots of questions. I think he left about an hour ago, maybe a little more."

An hour ago? He hadn't been in her room when she'd woken up.

Her stomach clenched with anxiety. So where was he?

CHAPTER NINE

SO THIS was it. The beginning of the end. Jadon was gone. Alyssa walked back to her room, trying not to feel overwhelmed by the concept of raising the girls all by herself.

When she crossed the threshold, she stopped, startled to see a huge bouquet of more than a dozen pink roses in a vase on her bedside table. There were also two pink "It's A Girl" balloons tied to the side-rail of her bed.

She read the small card tucked between the roses, feeling ashamed for doubting him when she realized the flowers and balloons were gifts from Jadon.

"Arranged some extra time off work, then ran home to get your suitcase. Be back soon, Jadon."

He hadn't left unexpectedly, other than to talk to his boss about having time off and to buy flowers and balloons. Ashamed, she realized she'd jumped to conclusions. He hadn't left her. He wasn't like her father. They must have just missed each other.

She counted eighteen blooms, stroking the velvet-soft petals with the tip of her index finger. Another first. Not quite as monumental as giving birth to twins, but she'd never received pink roses before. Or any other color roses. Not from Jadon or from anyone else.

He'd been so sweet and so supportive during the few hours she'd spent in labor, and afterward when they'd both been given the chance to hold their newly born daughters. She found it difficult to reconcile this new Jadon with the emotionally distant man who'd made love to her and then left without saying a word.

Let it go, she told herself. There's no reason to keep dwelling on the past. Jadon was here now, had gone as far as to ask her to move in with him. Maybe there was still some hope for them. Maybe he'd learn to show his feelings. Maybe she could trust him with her heart.

She was glad he'd gone to get her things.

Because she wouldn't mind wearing something other than the shapeless hospital gown to help her look a bit more attractive.

Jadon returned right after she finished with her dinner tray. "Do you want me to call the nurse to bring another tray for you?" she offered.

"No, thanks, I'm fine. I grabbed something quick right after I left." He set her small suitcase on the floor beside her bed.

"Thanks for the roses and the balloons," she said. "They were a nice surprise when I returned to my room after seeing Grace and Gretchen."

"You're welcome." He pulled up a chair beside her bed. "I spoke to Louis Downer, the neonatologist assigned to Grace and Gretch, and he really feels like the girls are doing amazingly well for being seven weeks early."

"I'm glad. Although I did try breast-feeding earlier and neither of the girls suckled for very long." She blushed when she noticed Jadon's gaze dropped to her breasts. Was he imagining how large and full her breasts were now? "The nurse told me the girls might need tube feedings."

Jadon nodded. "Yes, Louis mentioned that possibility to me as well. But tube feedings aren't the worst thing in the world. As long as they get nourishment and continue to grow, that's what really matters. Do you plan to, ah, continue nursing?"

She knew he was dancing around the issue of asking if she planned to pump her breasts to provide breast milk if the girls couldn't nurse on their own. "Yes, because at this point they need every possible advantage they can get."

"Very true." Jadon looked relieved at the news. "Louis warned me that both girls will likely need to be placed under the bili-lights, too. Even full-term babies sometimes need the bili-lights, but preemies even more so as their livers aren't fully developed yet."

"I know, I pretty much expected that." She'd learned a few things during her nursing school rotation through OB, but was hardly an expert.

"Alyssa, I think we need to talk about the future, maybe not right now but soon. Once you're discharged and back home." His serious, earnest gaze warmed her heart.

Home as in back at his house? She thought so. She saw his willingness to talk as a good sign. "I know."

"So that's settled," he said with satisfaction. "How about if we go and visit our daughters again?"

"I'd like that." She threw aside the blanket and

grimaced a little when she swung her legs over the side of the bed.

"Are you all right?" Jadon asked, noticing her discomfort. "Do you want me to get you a wheelchair?"

"No wheelchair, I'd rather walk." She bent down to grab the suitcase he'd brought in. "But first I need a few minutes in the bathroom."

"Sure." He relaxed in his chair, not seeming to be in the least bit impatient. "No rush."

In the bathroom she quickly changed into her own nightgown and robe, feeling a little better wearing her own things. The nightgown had a lace-tie in the front that would help if she tried nursing the girls again.

Jadon lightly clasped her hand as they walked down to the level-three nursery. Jadon led the way straight to Grace and Gretchen's isolettes.

"Are you here to hold your babies?" Carla asked, crossing over to them. "Let me grab a couple of warm blankets for you, all right?"

"Okay." Alyssa leaned forward, dividing her attention between both babies. "Aren't they cute, wearing those little pink hats?"

"They're adorable," Jadon agreed in a husky voice. "Beautiful, just like their mother."

Her heart swelled with love as she gazed at her daughters. Jadon had created these wonderful miracles with her. "Which one do you want to hold?" she asked him.

"I'll take Grace this time. I feel like we should alternate so we don't play favorites."

"I think it's a little early to worry about playing favorites," Alyssa said with a small laugh.

Carla returned with the warm blankets and quickly

wrapped up both babies and handed Grace to Jadon, and Gretchen to Alyssa.

They sat in side-by-side rockers, content to simply hold the babies.

"Lys?" Jadon said, glancing up at her. "You are going to come back home with me after you're discharged, right?"

"Yes." She frowned a little because she'd thought that was what he'd meant earlier.

"I knew you'd be discharged in the next day or two, but I also know that Louis thought the babies would be here for maybe a couple of weeks," Jadon explained. "So I wanted to make sure."

"A couple of weeks?" It was hard to hide her dismay. "He really thinks they'll need to stay that long? I was hoping we'd have them home by Christmas."

"Christmas is just over two weeks away, so don't be discouraged. We may get to take them home by then. Depending on how much weight they gain. And how well their breathing progresses."

"Alyssa?" Denise, her postpartum nurse, came into the nursery. "You have a couple of visitors, and there's one little boy especially who would like to see the babies."

"Kylie and Seth must have brought Ben," she said to Jadon before turning to Carla. "Do you think we could hold the babies up in the window for Ben to see? I'd hate to disappoint him."

"No problem," Carla said. "We'll just have to momentarily disconnect them from the monitors." At her panicked expression, Carla hastily reassured her. "Don't worry, we do that from time to time anyway, like to give them a bath. It's not a big deal for a few minutes."

"I'll bring the group over to the window," Denise said as she turned to leave the nursery.

Carla disconnected the twins from their monitors so that Alyssa and Jadon could hold the babies up in the window for Seth, Kylie and Ben to see.

"Wow, they're so tiny!" she heard Ben exclaim.

"Very tiny," Kylie agreed with a wide grin. "They're beautiful, Alyssa," she called through the glass.

"Thanks." She and Jadon only stayed for a minute, before turning back so that Carla could reconnect the babies to their monitors. Then they tucked the girls back into their isolettes and headed out to visit with Seth and Kylie.

"Hey, congrats to both of you," Seth said when they met up in the hall. He held out a hand to Jadon, who looked somewhat bemused as he accepted the handshake. Seth then turned to give Alyssa a hug. "You didn't call us," he complained in a light, teasing tone. "I had to hear the news from the ED staff."

"Yeah, and I thought I was supposed to be your birthing coach?" Kylie added, giving both Alyssa and Jadon a hug. "Looks like you did fine without me."

"I'm sorry, Kylie," Alyssa said. "Everything happened so fast."

Kylie rolled her eyes. "I'm only kidding, it's not a big deal. I'm just glad they're both doing all right."

"How come I can't hold the babies?" Ben wanted to know.

Alyssa reached down to give him a hug. "They're too little yet. We need to restrict visitors until the babies grow bigger and get stronger."

Ben looked disappointed.

"Ben, don't forget to give Alyssa the card you made for her," Kylie reminded him.

"Oh, yeah." He looked down at the rather crumpled piece of paper that he'd been clutching in his hand as if he'd forgotten all about it. "Here." He thrust it at Alyssa.

"Thank you, Ben. It's beautiful." He'd written a crooked "Congratulations, Alyssa" on the front with what she assumed were two babies in cribs and not tiny people in jail drawn on the bottom of the page. Inside the card he'd painstakingly penned a short message that she read out loud. "'Thanks for saving my life. I love you, Ben.'"

For a moment the words swam in her vision as her eyes misted. She drew him close for another hug. "This is my favorite card in the whole world, Ben. Thanks so much."

"Welcome," he muttered, giving her a tight hug and then breaking away, his attention already moving to the next thing. "Can we get something out of the vending machine, Mom?"

Seth and Kylie exchanged a questioning glance and when Kylie nodded, Seth dug several quarters out of his pocket. "Sure, here you go, sport."

"Cool!" Ben dashed off.

"Jadon, I picked up your Saturday-night shift for you," Seth informed him.

"Thanks." Jadon looked pleasantly surprised. "I appreciate it."

"No problem." Seth shrugged it off but Alyssa knew the gesture was a peace offering. She and Kylie exchanged knowing grins.

Shortly after Ben returned, Kylie and Seth prepared to leave. After they left, promising to return for another visit soon, Jadon stood, too. "I'd better let you get some rest."

She masked her disappointment, knowing there was no reason for Jadon to stay overnight. She was fine. Gracie and Gretchen were fine. He deserved a good night's sleep, which he wouldn't get sleeping on a recliner in her room.

"All right. Get some sleep," she told him.

"You, too." He leaned over and kissed her. For a moment their lips clung and then he deepened the kiss, exploring her mouth in a way that made her breathless when he finally lifted his head.

"See you tomorrow," he promised in a husky voice.

She relaxed against the pillows, her lips tingling from his kiss, and nodded.

This time she believed him.

"Simon, are you off work yet?" Jadon demanded over his cell phone. It was late, eleven-thirty at night, and he'd been waiting impatiently for Simon's call. "I need your help."

"Yes, I just finished, we had another busy night. Why? What's up?"

"I'm at Alyssa's apartment. I need your help to move the two cribs, the baby swings, the dressers, and everything else that she has here in her storage bin to my place."

Simon let out a heavy sigh. "Where in the heck are you going to put all that stuff?" he asked.

"At my house," Jadon repeated as if he were a tad slow. "I rented the truck again this afternoon so I have most of the stuff loaded in there already, except those two baby dressers because they're darned heavy."

"I'll be right there," Simon said in a resigned tone.

Jadon knew he'd set an almost impossible task, getting the bedroom totally painted and the furniture all set up as a surprise for Alyssa once she was discharged from the hospital. Yet he also knew he'd get it done, even if he had to stay up all night.

Simon arrived and they carried the two baby dressers down to the truck. Once they arrived at Jadon's house, he elicited Simon's help to take apart Alyssa's bedroom set.

His friend placed his hands on his hips. "But if we take Alyssa's bed down, where is she going to sleep?" he asked with feigned innocence.

Jadon sent him a narrow glance. "Ha, ha. Very funny. Give me a hand, will you?"

"Okay, but remember it was only a couple of days ago that you asked me to help you put it together in the first place."

He grimaced. "I know. But we didn't plan on having the girls seven weeks early either."

"Listen to you," Simon said as he took a screwdriver and attacked the bed frame. "You sound like an old married man."

His words made Jadon's stomach clench. He still wasn't sure how he was going to handle things, but somehow he'd make it work. He didn't really have a choice. "Alyssa's going to be thrilled to see this," he said. "I'm painting the walls pink."

"Pink?" Simon's gaze was skeptical. "You might reconsider. You're going to get sick of pink with two girls."

"Never." Jadon grinned as he hauled the mattresses

out of the room. He was going to store Alyssa's bedroom set down in the basement for now. Simon had already helped him haul all the baby stuff inside, so maneuvering through the living room with the mattresses wasn't easy.

He didn't mind. He already had everything all planned out. Once Alyssa had been discharged from the hospital he'd bring her here to see the nursery he'd made for their daughters and then he'd tell her the truth about his brother.

The answer to his problems was simple. He could keep his dysfunctional family separate from his new one. With this arrangement, he could minimize the stress of Jack's illness for Alyssa and the girls.

This could work.

The next day Jadon didn't show up until almost noon, and even then he looked awful, ragged and exhausted as if he hadn't gotten much sleep.

"What happened?" Alyssa asked in alarm. "Did you get called in to work?"

"No, I just had trouble sleeping, that's all." He yawned widely, but then opened his eyes wide as if to prove he was really awake. "It's not a big deal. I'm fine."

She wasn't so sure. What on earth had kept him up all night? It wasn't as if there was anything to worry about or to stress over.

Except being a father.

Her stomach tightened. That had to be it. Was he having second thoughts about asking her to stay with him? Was the stress going to eventually get to him, making him leave? Did Jadon really want a fully committed relationship? Or was he already backing off?

She needed to stop imagining the worst.

"Have you seen the babies yet today?" he asked, changing the subject.

"Yes. I tried to nurse again this morning, but they didn't do very well again. So I learned all about the breast pump." She made a face.

"I thought it took a few days for your milk to come in?" he asked, as if having a detailed conversation about breast-feeding was perfectly natural.

Which didn't give the impression he was having second thoughts.

"It does. But the colostrum that's there before the milk comes in is very good for the babies, too, and my milk won't come in unless I nurse." Darn it, she could feel her cheeks getting warm again. Why was she embarrassed? Their tentative relationship seemed to be going well; there was no reason for her to overreact like this.

"And they're still breathing fine on their own?"

She nodded. "Yes, even Gretchen, although she seems to be having more of that apneic breathing that they're so concerned about. Grace has it, too, but I guess Gretchen's percentages are a little higher."

"Hmm. Something to ask Louis about, I guess. Do you mind if we go down to see them again?" Jadon asked. "Or if you're too tired, I can go myself."

"I'm not too tired," she assured him, getting up out of bed. She was moving much better today and, as Kim had promised, was hardly sore at all. She'd spent over two hours in the level-three nursery that morning, but she didn't mind going again.

Soon the babies would be her responsibility, full-time. Jadon would help, but she'd still better get used to it.

"Do you realize the girls are now a little more than twenty-four hours old?" Jadon announced as they made their way down the hall.

She had to smile. "Yes, I know. I was there, too, remember?"

"It's just so amazing." He took her hand again and she reveled in the closeness as they made their way through to the nursery.

This time she took Grace and Jadon took Gretchen. Although Gretchen was very sleepy, they traded off after a while.

Louis Downer came in to make rounds while they were there. "Hi, Jadon. Alyssa, how are you feeling today?"

"I'm fine, although I'm a little worried about how the girls still aren't suckling very much," she admitted.

"I know. But we'll give them tube feedings so they'll still grow fine." He glanced at the babies they held in their respective grasps. "Which one is Gretchen?"

"I have Gretchen," Alyssa said. "Why?"

"I'd like to examine her first. Her chest X-ray didn't look as good as I would have liked this morning."

Alarmed, she glanced at Jadon as she handed the infant to the neonatologist. "Do you think she's sick?"

"Just something to keep an eye on," he assured her, as he took the tiny twin. He gently set her back in her isolette, and then unwrapped the blanket from around her chest so he could listen. After he'd removed the stethoscope from his ears, he picked up her clipboard and reviewed her vital signs.

Alyssa craned her neck, so she could see, too.

"Well?" Jadon asked, when Louis set the clipboard aside and turned back toward them.

"She's started to run a slight fever," Louis admitted. "I'm going to treat her with IV antibiotics because I suspect she's showing early signs of pneumonia."

CHAPTER TEN

JADON wanted to reassure Alyssa that Gretchen would be all right, but it was difficult to put aside his own fears. She was so tiny, it was hard to imagine how her immune system would fight off something as serious as pneumonia. And there was the additional concern about how well her premature kidneys would tolerate the antibiotics. Not to mention how she'd maintain her oxygenation levels with lungs full of infection.

There was no doubt the next twenty-four hours would be critical for Gretchen.

And there was nothing he could do to help her.

Alyssa refused to leave. Watching her keeping vigil over Gretchen was difficult. After several hours Jadon had had enough. "You need some rest," he pointed out in a low tone. "And it's close to dinnertime. Let's go back to your room."

"No. I want to stay here." Alyssa had been staring at the monitor over Gretchen's isolette for so long she was starting to look like a zombie. It was as if her emotions had completely shut down. He understood how she felt—he'd always done the same thing when faced with one of Jack's crises, shutting away the pain so it couldn't hurt. Still, he didn't like the idea of Alyssa sitting by the girls' isolettes all night long.

"Alyssa, look at me," he demanded in a sharp tone, breaking through her zombie-like stare.

Reluctantly, she turned to meet his gaze, her eyes dull with resigned acceptance.

"Wearing yourself to the brink of exhaustion isn't good for you or for Grace. We have two daughters, remember? You need to eat, to keep up your strength and your nutrition, as you've told me you want to continue to provide breast milk for them."

Alyssa slowly nodded, as if agreeing with him. But she didn't move to leave.

He intended to keep pushing, to do what was best no matter what it took. He reached down, grasped her hand and tugged her to her feet. "Let's go. We need to head back to your room."

For a heart-stopping moment Alyssa looked as if she might burst into tears, but she allowed herself to be drawn upright. "You're right. I know you are. But I just can't bear to leave her. What if something happens while we're gone?"

He understood her angst because he felt it, too. He pulled her into his arms, enfolding her in a warm hug. "I know it's difficult to leave, but she'll be okay."

Alyssa didn't push him away as he half expected, but clung to him, burying her face against his chest, as if she couldn't stand under her own power. He could feel the dampness of her tears soaking his shirt. He held her close for countless minutes as he silently offered his strength and support, drawing strength from her closeness as well.

It was much easier to face the hardship together.

Although hardships also had the power to drag people apart, too.

Finally she drew a ragged breath and lifted her head. "Do you think Carla will call us if anything changes?"

He lifted his hands to cradle her face, using his thumbs to wipe away her tears. "Yes, I know she will. But I honestly think Gretchen is going to be fine. Louis Downer is a good doctor. Our daughter is getting the best care available. Besides, Gretch is a fighter. She'll be fine, you'll see."

"She barely weighs three pounds," Alyssa murmured, swinging around to stare down at Gretchen lying in her isolette. Both babies had lost a few ounces after the delivery, which was completely normal.

"I know," he soothed, despite the grim certainty of knowing there were no guarantees. "But think about all these other tiny babies, most of them less than three pounds, and they're doing all right."

Alyssa's mouth turned up in a watery smile. "They are all very tiny, aren't they? You're right, Gretchen is one of the larger babies in here. She'll fight this and win."

"Of course she will." He slid his arm around her waist, turning her slowly away from the babies and encouraging her to walk along with him out of the nursery.

"How did she get pneumonia so quickly?" she fretted as they made their way back to her room.

"She was in utero longer than Grace," he reminded her. "Maybe she aspirated during the delivery."

He'd heard the story about his and Jack's birth and the circumstances were eerily similar to those of Grace and Gretchen. Except he'd been the smaller, younger baby, in fact, much smaller than Gretchen.

He slammed a door on those wayward thoughts. The last thing he wanted to do was to draw comparisons between his daughters and how events had unfolded between him and his brother. There were plenty of neonates who got sick. A little pneumonia wasn't the end of the world.

And no matter what, he was going to pay attention to both of his children—focusing on their strengths and offering encouragement no matter how different their personalities.

He managed to keep Alyssa resting in her room for a full hour while they ate dinner, but when they'd finished, she insisted on returning to the nursery.

He accompanied her back to see Grace and Gretchen, noting the nursing staff had been required to change Gretchen's IV site already because her other one had blown. Knowing it was a common occurrence for infants didn't make looking at her bruised yet delicate skin any easier.

"Poor Gretch," Alyssa murmured.

"Let me hold her for a while," he said to the nurse. "I'll keep her in the isolette as she's getting another dose of antibiotics, but I'll cradle her in my hands for a bit."

"Of course," Carla said, gesturing to the isolette. "Go right ahead. The more you hold her, the more she'll become used to your scent and your touch."

"I know." He gently lifted a listless Gretchen off the blanket, drawing the tip of his finger down the side of her cheek in a slight caress.

He'd tried to be strong for Alyssa, but as he stared down at Gretchen, he silently prayed his tiny daughter would make it through unscathed. That she'd not only make it over this hurdle of pneumonia but also over all the other hurdles she'd face throughout her life.

There were some things he couldn't do for her. And fighting off this infection was one of those things. There would be others as well.

The responsibility of fatherhood weighed heavily on his shoulders.

Alyssa had to bite her lip hard to prevent herself from crying out as Dr. Downer placed a tiny CPAP mask over Gretchen's face, the device totally engulfing her cute button nose and perfectly formed mouth. The apparatus seemed overly large and invasive against her tiny, dainty features.

Her daughter was sick. Very sick. And she couldn't simply tell herself Gretchen would get through this, because she wasn't certain she would.

How could such a small baby fight off a life-threatening infection?

And why wouldn't Jadon talk about his feelings?

Later that night, she followed Jadon back to her room. He stayed for a while, but then went home for a bit. When he left, she slipped out of bed and went back to the nursery.

The neonatal nurses looked at her with kind empathy, suggesting she needed to get some sleep, but she ignored their advice.

What if the mask didn't work? She was too afraid Gretchen was going to need a breathing tube in her lungs and be placed on a ventilator.

"It's after midnight, Ms. Knight," Evie, the night nurse, said in her soft, quiet voice. "You really should go back to your room to get some rest."

"Are you telling me I have to leave?" Alyssa asked sharply, annoyed by the nurse's prodding. "I was under the impression I could stay for as long as I wanted."

Evie's eyes widened at her vehement tone. "Not at all, but wearing yourself out isn't good for you either. I'm only concerned about your welfare."

Alyssa closed her eyes and took a deep breath. She shouldn't have snapped, but in that moment the night-shift nurse had sounded so much like Jadon she hadn't been able to help her response.

"I'm sorry," she murmured to Evie. "I'll leave, soon."

Her anger wasn't really aimed at the nurse but toward Jadon. Over the past few hours she'd realized she resented how easily he'd gone home, leaving her here all alone. Granted, he'd been exhausted, and she'd noticed how he'd tossed and turned in the recliner. Still, she'd wanted him to stay.

Slowly she rose to her feet, understanding Evie was right. If she didn't get some rest, she wouldn't be any help to Grace or Gretchen.

If only Jadon were still here with her. Maybe then she wouldn't have felt so alone.

The next morning, the uncomfortable tautness in her breasts confirmed her milk was coming in.

Good news that she'd be able to provide healthy nourishment for Gracie and Gretchen.

Especially Gretchen, who needed the extra boost now more than ever.

She went to the nursery for more attempts at nursing, and Grace did suckle for almost ten minutes, a record for the little one, but Gretchen was still wearing her mask, so nursing wasn't an option.

She used the breast pump to provide milk for Gretchen's tube feedings, taking time to hold the baby close for some additional bonding.

Kim showed up in her room after she'd finished with the girls.

"Good morning, how are you doing today?" Kim asked.

Alyssa's smile was strained. "Fair, although I'd be much better if Gretchen's pneumonia would clear up."

"I know." Kim's expression softened as she continued, "You know, according to hospital policy, I'm supposed to discharge you today. However, considering Gretchen's tenuous condition, and the fact that you're breast-feeding, I could probably extend your stay one more day."

She sucked in a quick, hopeful breath. "Really? You could do that for me?"

"Yes. I think I could make it work so your insurance will cover the extra day, too."

"That would be wonderful," Alyssa admitted. "Not that I'm thrilled with the idea of staying here in the hospital rather than being home in my own bed, but I really want to be close to the girls for a little while longer."

"I understand," Kim said with a smile. "Leaving your babies here while you go home is probably going to be difficult. And I can only promise one more day. Just remember you can come in to visit anytime."

"Thanks, Dr. Rayborn," she said gratefully. "I really do appreciate the extra time."

"No problem. Please pay attention to your own body, too, though. You did just give birth and we need to make sure you're fully healed as well. How have you been doing? Everything all right? No aches or pains, or problems that you might not have paid attention to?"

She hid a wince, knowing all her attention had been centered on Grace and Gretchen. She thought back over the past few days. "Well, now that you mention it, I did notice a little burning last night when I emptied my bladder."

Kim arched a brow. "Hmm. Maybe you have a bladder infection. We'll send a sample to the lab and start you on antibiotics."

"Antibiotics?" she echoed in alarm. This was exactly why she hadn't said anything right away. "But I'm breast-feeding. I don't want to take anything that will harm the babies. Why don't we wait to see if the infection will clear up on its own? I'll drink extra cranberry juice, I promise."

"Cranberry juice is a good idea, but I don't want to take any chances. The antibiotic is very mild and it won't hurt the babies at all," Kim reassured her. "Don't worry."

"Okay," she reluctantly agreed.

Jadon returned to the hospital earlier than the day before and at least he looked better, not nearly as tired and exhausted as the day before.

"Good morning," he greeted her with a smile. "Has Kim been in yet? Are you officially discharged?"

"Kim has been in, but I'm not going to be discharged

today," she told him. "Turns out I have a bladder infection, for one thing. And she thought as Gretchen is so sick, she could work it out so that I can stay for another day."

"Oh." Was that a flash of disappointment in his eyes? "Well, it's good that you can be close to Grace and Gretchen for another day."

"Are you ready to see the girls?" she asked, swinging her legs out of bed. "My milk has come in, so I was able to nurse Grace this morning, but Gretchen had to settle for tube feedings."

"Sure." He smiled again, and took her hand as they went down the hall toward the nursery.

When they arrived, though, Dr. Downer was standing in front of Gretchen's isolette with his stethoscope dangling from around his neck, discussing something intently with a nurse. Her stomach clenched in warning.

"Something's wrong," she murmured.

Jadon gave her hand a reassuring squeeze. "Maybe not. It's possible she's doing better and they're discussing taking off the mask."

"Maybe." But she didn't think so. For one thing, Dr. Downer's expression seemed too serious. And so was Renee's.

"Hi, Alyssa, Jadon," Louis greeted them when they came closer. "You're just in time. We've been discussing Gretchen's breathing."

Alyssa's mouth went dry. "Is there something wrong? Isn't the CPAP mask helping her lungs?"

"It's helping," Louis said hesitantly, "but I'm not sure it's helping enough. Her chest X-ray this morning doesn't look much better and her pulse ox is hanging in the low nineties." He shook his head. "I'd like to see her oxygen percentage up higher than that."

The knot in her stomach tightened. "How?"

"First we're going to give her a few breathing treatments and another dose of IV antibiotics."

"And if that doesn't work?" Jadon asked.

"Then we'd need to place a breathing tube in her lungs and put her on a ventilator," Louis admitted. "We'll try to hold off, using the breathing tube as a last resort. And if we do put it in, we probably won't need to keep it in very long. I promise we'll take it out the moment Gretchen doesn't need it anymore."

Alyssa didn't know what to say. She didn't want Gretchen to have the breathing tube; she knew there were all sorts of potential complications that went along with it. Yet not having enough oxygen in her blood available to all her vital organs like her heart, brain and kidneys could also create problems.

"Can I hold her for a while?" she asked Renee.

"Sure, but keep her in the isolette if you can."

Holding Gretchen in the palms of her hands wasn't nearly as rewarding as holding her against her heart, but she was determined to spend as much time with Gretchen as possible.

Renee and Louis left them alone. Alyssa found she couldn't tear her eyes away from Gretchen, her brain already imagining what she'd look like with a breathing tube in.

"You can't ignore Grace," Jadon chided. "I know Gretchen is sick, but Grace deserves your love and attention, too."

His slightly accusing, brusque tone grated on her

nerves. "I was here this morning, nursing Grace. You're the one who went home last night. Don't lecture me. If anyone hasn't been spending enough time with Grace, it's you."

For a long moment antagonistic tension shimmered in the air between them.

Jadon turned away first, letting out a harsh breath and plowing his fingers through his hair. "I'm sorry. You're right. I have no right to lecture you."

His apology caught her off guard, and she realized this was their first fight. Ever. When Jadon had left so unexpectedly, she hadn't been given a chance to argue with him. You had to care about something, have feelings to argue.

She was inexplicably encouraged by his outburst. He'd proved he wasn't as emotionally distant from the situation with Gretchen as she'd thought.

"It's okay," she said slowly. "I shouldn't have snapped. I guess I've been on edge lately, too."

Jadon nodded. "We both have. Obviously there's been a lot to deal with in a very short period of time."

They took turns holding the girls, switching the babies, declaring a wordless truce to support each other during this time of crisis. Jadon seemed less remote after their disagreement.

Alyssa hoped that surviving their first fight was a good sign of their evolving relationship. Fighting meant having feelings.

Maybe there was hope for their future after all.

CHAPTER ELEVEN

ALYSSA and Jadon both stayed in the nursery until almost midnight again, relieved when Gretchen seemed to be holding her own on the CPAP mask.

So far she hadn't needed a breathing tube and Alyssa could only hope and pray that Gretchen was on the cusp of doing better, her pneumonia clearing up so she soon wouldn't need assistance with her breathing at all.

She was glad Jadon had decided to stay with her this time, instead of going home. Even if the recliner did look awfully uncomfortable.

When she finally awoke the next morning, she was distressed to see Jadon was already gone. Was he visiting the babies? Or had he left to run home?

She missed him. Sleeping beside him, being held by him when she'd been upset about Gretch. He'd been a rock during this very emotionally draining time. So far he wasn't giving her the impression he was going to cut and run when things got tough.

How on earth had she imagined she'd be able to raise these two girls by herself? Especially given that she'd had the twins prematurely? Who else would she have leaned on when Gretchen had got sick?

Her friends? Seth and Kylie? Maybe, but not likely. Not the way she'd leaned on Jadon.

And how had her mother managed?

She had no idea. Her mother was more of a saint than she'd given her credit for.

After climbing out of bed, she hurried down to the nursery to attempt to breast-feed Grace. She'd expected to see Jadon there, but he'd been in and had already gone. Trying not to be disappointed, she rocked and fed Grace, silently acknowledging that maybe she hadn't been entirely fair in her assessment of her mother's ability to adapt to being a single mother.

It wasn't exactly her mother's fault that she hadn't attended college. Her mother had fallen pregnant during her first year of college and had been forced to drop out of her classes. She'd tried going back for evening sessions, but had stopped altogether when Alyssa's oh, so charming father had disappeared from the picture for good.

Maybe they hadn't had a lot of money while she'd been growing up, but certainly they'd had love. Maybe her mother hadn't shown love as much as she'd wanted, but they had shared some wonderful, very special Christmases. And if they'd moved around a lot, from one seemingly better job to another, at least Alyssa hadn't gone hungry.

Constantly making new friends hadn't been easy, and that had been why once she'd come to Cedar Bluff she'd immediately fallen in love with the town. The people were exceptionally nice and friendly. From the very first she'd felt as if she'd come home.

If she hadn't experienced the nomadic upbringing she had, she might never have found Cedar Bluff.

Or Jadon.

She smiled down at Grace, who'd suckled hungrily that morning at her breast. Grace was by far the stronger and healthier of the twins. Gretchen still wore the mask, but Alyssa told herself that was better than coming in to find her on a ventilator.

Once Grace had taken her fill, which admittedly wasn't a lot, Alyssa used the breast pump so she could freeze the extra milk for both twins and then spent some time holding Gretchen.

Leaving the nursery, she returned to her room to eat her own breakfast and to wait for Kim to come and formally discharge her. While she knew this would mean spending less time with the girls, she was anxious to get back home.

Not to her apartment, but to Jadon's house.

"Good morning," Kim greeted her cheerfully as she entered the room. "Are you ready to go home?"

"Absolutely," she agreed, although she thought it was odd that Jadon hadn't returned. Where was he?

"And how is your bladder? Are you still experiencing some burning when you go?"

"Nope, that's all fine."

"Good. That means the antibiotics are helping." Kim made a few notes on her clipboard. "All right, then, you're free to leave. I have a prescription here for your antibiotics. You can get it filled right here at our outpatient pharmacy."

"Sounds good." She took the prescription Kim held out. "Thanks again for everything."

"You're very welcome," Kim said with a smile. "Don't forget, no sexual activity for a while, until you feel up to it. And you'll need to come and see me in six weeks."

"I will." Alyssa put the prescription near her purse and reached for her suitcase. Once Kim had left, she changed out of her nightgown and into the clean clothes Jadon had brought for her.

She was disappointed that she still needed to wear her maternity clothes. All the nurses had assured her she'd lose the extra weight faster if she breast-fed the babies and she really hoped they were right. Not that Jadon had said a word about her pudgy shape, but she still wanted to get back into her old clothes.

And where was Jadon? She frowned and then decided there was no need to sit here and wonder about Jadon. She should spend every minute she could with the girls instead.

On the way to the nursery, though, she abruptly stopped as an idea occurred to her. Maybe Jadon had been called in to work. He'd been off for several days already so she certainly understood if he needed to pick up a shift.

She turned and headed down to the emergency department to see if he was there, working. The charge nurse on duty would know which attending physicians were scheduled to work.

The ED was bustling with activity when she walked into the arena. Muted Christmas music was playing through the loudspeaker, but the tunes could barely be heard through the normal sounds of monitors beeping, staff talking and the occasional patient yelling.

Wistfully, she glanced around, realizing she missed the place. As soon as a few of her nursing colleagues saw her, they rushed over.

"Alyssa! How are you? How are the twins?" Susan asked, reaching her first and giving her a quick hug.

"We heard you have two girls," Melanie added, coming up behind Susan.

"I'm fine and the twins are fine, too," she said with a laugh. "Their names are Grace and Gretchen, and of course they are the most beautiful babies in the whole nursery."

"Of course they are," Susan agreed staunchly. "What are you doing down here? Looking for Theresa?"

Theresa Williams was their nurse manager and with a shock Alyssa realized she hadn't exactly kept her boss informed of the events surrounding her delivery.

"I should probably talk to Theresa," Alyssa agreed, glancing around the arena. "Do you know where she is?"

"I think she's in her office," Melanie said helpfully. "But if not, we can have her paged."

"Thanks. I'll chat with you both later." Alyssa hurried to her boss's office, spending a few minutes going over the terms of her medical leave of absence. She felt a sense of relief when she'd finished all the paperwork, including the form she needed to complete in order to add her infant daughters to her health insurance plan.

Considering the bill they were running up in the nursery, it was a good thing she'd stopped by or she might have forgotten all about it.

"By the way, which physician is on duty tonight?" she asked her boss.

"Let me check." Theresa pulled up her computerized physician schedule. "Unless there have been any changes, Dr. Carter is on for the second shift and Dr. Taylor is on for third shift."

So Jadon wasn't on the schedule, not even on third shift. Unless either Simon or Seth had called him to cover their hours at the last minute.

Trying not to dwell on where Jadon might be, she left Theresa's office. As she walked past the trauma bay, she noticed there were two trauma resuscitations going on at the same time, and curiosity caused her to stop to watch for a few minutes. It quickly became apparent that the two victims had been involved in the same crash.

"Here's the chest X-ray you asked for, Dr. Torres."

An attractive, tall, dark-haired, rather European-looking doctor glanced at the computer image of the film and turned back to the patient. "This guy's left lung is collapsed," he said in a sharp tone. "I need to insert a chest tube, stat."

Maureen, the new trainee she'd worked with a week ago, was rummaging through the trauma resuscitation cart, anxiously looking for the chest tube he'd asked for.

Alyssa didn't recognize Dr. Torres, but as Maureen was looking in the wrong places for the tube, she darted in and opened the correct drawer. "Here," she said, pulling out the chest tube and handing it to her. "Drawer six for chest tubes and instruments."

"Thanks," Maureen said in obvious relief. Evidently, the new physician had her on edge. "Here you go, Dr. Torres."

He took the chest tube, but then his attention centered on Alyssa. "Who are you?" he demanded. "If you're not a part of this resuscitation team, get out or I'll call Security."

Alyssa glanced around, but realized with a shock

that he was actually talking to her. Not that he didn't have every right to question who she was, as she obviously wasn't wearing the proper attire or her ID tag, but his threat to contact Security seemed a bit extreme. Hadn't she just helped out a coworker? What was his problem?

"I'm sorry," she started to apologize, but Leila Ross, one of the trauma surgeons, quickly came to her rescue.

"Alyssa Knight is one of our ED nurses—there's no reason to call Security." By the acid contempt in her tone, it was easy to deduce that Leila didn't particularly care for the new physician. "Thanks for your help, Alyssa. We're fine now."

"Sure," she murmured, taking the hint and stepping out of the trauma area. She glanced at Dr. Torres, but he'd apparently already forgotten about her, his attention centered on placing the chest tube in his patient.

She headed back toward the arena, where she ran into Susan. "The traumas are two snowmobile riders who hit each other head-on. I bet you're glad to be out of here for a few months, huh?" Susan asked, coming up beside her. "Good way to escape the craziness around here."

She thought dealing with premature twins would have its own element of craziness, but didn't respond. Susan brushed past, heading into the trauma room to offer more help, and Alyssa watched, wishing she had a chance to ask about the new doctor on staff.

Not that it mattered much, since, as Susan had pointed out, she'd be off for a few months. Hopefully by the time she was scheduled to return, Dr. Torres would have forgotten all about this little incident.

She turned and left, heading back upstairs to the

nursery, knowing she'd miss the excitement of the ED to a certain extent. Taking care of patients had always been her passion. Yet she was also a mother now, and her precious, tiny, preemie daughters had to come first.

Half expecting to run into Jadon, she was disappointed to note he wasn't waiting for her in the nursery. Where in the heck was he? Surely he hadn't forgotten she was being discharged today?

Her ire faded when she looked at Gretchen and noticed the CPAP mask had been removed from her daughter.

"Renee?" she called to the day-shift nurse, who was standing nearby. "Why is Gretchen's mask off? Is she doing better?"

"Yes, Gretchen is doing much better," Renee confirmed, crossing over to her with a reassuring smile. "As a matter of fact, Dr. Downer was just here looking for you and Jadon. Why don't I page him?"

"Please. I'd love to talk to him." Alyssa wished Jadon was here, too, so the doctor could talk to both of them. They should be able to share the good news along with the bad.

"Alyssa, I'm glad you're here. Gretchen's chest X-ray looks remarkably improved so we're doing a trial to see how well she's oxygenating with the CPAP mask off." He glanced at the monitor over Gretchen's isolette and waved a hand at the pulse ox reading. "She's at ninety-five percent, which means so far she's holding her own."

"Really?" She was almost afraid to hope. "You really think she won't need the mask again?"

"I think between the antibiotics and the extra nutrition she's been getting, little Gretchen is going to be just fine," he assured her. "But we'll watch her closely, just in case."

Hope swelled, filling her heart with joyous relief. She knew they would keep a close eye on Gretchen, and on Grace. She was lucky to have such a great team of caregivers for her babies. "I'm so glad."

"Me, too. I understand you're going to be discharged today, is that correct?" he asked.

"Yes, but you can contact me on my cell phone if there's any changes with Grace or Gretch." She recited the number, patting her pockets and belatedly realizing the device was still in her suitcase. Jadon had thought of everything when he'd packed the bag for her, including her cell phone. "And I'll be here for a little while yet." Thankfully Jadon lived close to the hospital, so she could come and visit the girls often.

"Great. For now there isn't much else for us to do except to take good care of the babies and watch to be sure they don't have any other complications while they gain weight," he said.

"Sounds good." Excited, she took Gretchen out of her isolette to hold her close to her breast for the first time since the mask had gone on.

It seemed like forever. But after she'd held Gretchen, she gave Grace a nuzzle, too, unable to stop smiling.

Gretchen was doing okay. Soon the girls would be able to come home.

Which meant she needed to get ready for them.

After visiting for another hour, Alyssa walked back down to her room, becoming more vexed with Jadon.

It was past noon. Why wasn't he back by now? What on earth could be so important?

"Alyssa?" Denise flagged her down. "Jadon has been trying to get in touch with you."

"He has?" she asked with a frown. "Where is he?"

Denise lifted her shoulder in a slight shrug. "I'm not sure, but he would like you to call him on his cell phone. I wrote the number down for you."

Good thing, as she didn't have Jadon's new cell-phone number. She didn't even have his old cell-phone number anymore. She took the slip of paper and returned to her room. Picking up her phone from her suitcase, she saw there were several missed calls.

And the battery was almost flat, so she used the phone in her hospital room to call him. "Jadon, it's Alyssa. I just got your message," she said when he answered.

"Alyssa, I've been trying to reach you. I won't be able to take you home today."

A warning chill snaked down her spine. "Why not? Where are you?"

There was a slight pause, as if he was trying to figure out exactly what to say. "I had to leave early this morning for another family crisis. You were sleeping, so I didn't want to wake you. I should be back later tonight. Traffic is awful so I can't get into it now. I promise I'll explain later."

She sank onto the edge of her bed, staring out her window at the snow-covered trees surrounding Cedar Bluff Hospital. Looking at the wintry landscape, it made her all the more aware of the coldness she felt inside. "You left town," she said dully.

"Yes. But not for long. I'll be back soon."

Now it was soon, when earlier he'd claimed he'd be home later that night. So which was it?

She had a bad feeling he didn't know.

"So what am I supposed to do? Go back to my apartment and sleep on my couch?" Her bedroom set just happened to be set up at Jadon's house.

"I left a key to my place with Simon. He's working second shift tonight, and he's going to stop by the hospital to give you the key. If you want him to give you a lift to my place, I'm sure he will, but if you're going to sit and visit with the girls anyway, you may as well wait there for me. It's your choice."

Her choice? What if she wanted option number three—none of the above? What if she wanted Jadon to forget about his family crisis because they were having their own family crisis here?

There wasn't any choice. Jadon had already made it by leaving.

"Fine," she said woodenly, unable to hide the depth of her disappointment and discouragement. She wasn't sure she could stand going back to Jadon's house under these circumstances, although the idea of going to her small apartment wasn't much better. "Call me when you get back into town."

"I will." There was another pause, as if he wanted to say something more, but he only added, "Take care."

She closed her eyes and whispered, "You, too," before hanging up the phone.

The bitter taste of resentment nearly choked her. She buried her face in her hands to stave off the threat of tears burning the back of her throat. She should be glad he'd called her this time, instead of simply taking off without a word, but she wasn't.

Because Jadon hadn't mentioned anything about either of his daughters.

He'd been to the nursery earlier that morning but had left without knowing Gretchen had taken a turn for the better. From the way Dr. Downer had found her to give her the update on Gretchen, she knew he hadn't already talked to Jadon over the phone.

For all Jadon knew, his tiny daughter could still be fighting for her life.

And she couldn't believe his family crisis could be more important than his own daughter.

CHAPTER TWELVE

JADON closed his cell phone, feeling sick to his stomach.
Could his brother's timing be any worse? Alyssa was
upset, not that he could blame her. He should have dis-
cussed everything with her sooner.

Although reliving the past hadn't been much of a
priority, not with everything going on in the present.

He'd gotten up early and had gone to the nursery to
check on Gretchen, but then his mother had called. He
didn't want his mother to be hurt by Jack's outbursts
like she had in the past, so he'd promised to come, even
though he'd wanted to stay with Alyssa and Gretchen.
But what choice did he have?

Jack needed him. He'd wanted to refuse to rush to
the rescue, but he couldn't ignore Jack's problems.

Not when they were inadvertently at least partially
his fault.

His mother lived in the same small house they'd
grown up in, located in the rural part of Madison,
Wisconsin. She'd stayed after she and his father had
divorced. The trip took a couple of hours by car. When
he finally pulled into his mother's driveway, he was

shocked to discover there were several cars there. Jack's for one. But what about the others?

When he strode up to his house, he was even more surprised to recognize his father standing beside his mother. From the way they were talking, his father had just arrived, too.

His parents had split up when he and Jack had been teenagers, the strain of Jack's illness having been too much to hold their marriage together. Jadon hadn't seen his father in years, especially after he'd remarried. His new stepmother hadn't liked dealing with Jack's illness either.

So why was he back? He wasn't sure, but he didn't have time to sort it all out now. His mother stood in the kitchen, obviously upset, wringing her hands.

"Where is he?" he asked, barely glancing at his father.

"Upstairs. He's locked himself in your old bedroom."

He raked her with a gaze, searching for any sign of injury. "Are you all right? Did he hurt you?"

"I'm fine." His mother's strain was evident in her falsely positive tone. "But I'm worried about him, Jadon. He seemed to be doing so well, and now this."

"I know. I'll go up there to try talking to him, but you'll have to call the police, just in case."

Clearly his mother didn't like that idea. He'd told her to call the police earlier, too, when she'd first called him, but she hadn't listened.

"I don't want him to be arrested again," she protested in a low voice.

He suppressed a sigh. "Neither do I, but we may need them to help control him." Last time Jack had almost killed himself, which was bad enough. But his unpredictable behavior was also a threat to those around him. Jadon wasn't taking any chances.

His father was surprisingly silent during their brief conversation, but now he stood and headed for the phone. "I'll call the police."

Grateful, Jadon gave him a brief nod and then headed upstairs, hearing thuds coming from their old bedroom as Jack paced. His brother always paced when he was upset. Jadon heard Jack talking to himself, sounding agitated and making threats.

A wave of helplessness washed over him. None of this was Jack's fault, not really. His brother was sick with a mental illness. It just didn't seem fair that some people struggled with so much inner turmoil while others didn't.

There was a crash as something hit the floor. Oh, boy. He drew a deep breath and knocked at the door. "Jack? It's me, Jadon. I'm here to help. Unlock the door and let me in."

Jack's voice got louder. "No. Leave me alone. Just leave me the hell alone."

Jadon pressed his palm flat against the door, knowing he could break through the flimsy frame with a solid kick if he had to. But that would only rile his brother, putting him on the defensive. He maintained his calm approach. "Jack, please. I want to help. Let me in."

There was no answer, but then the door swung open and his identical twin stood there regarding him with bloodshot eyes. Jack looked awful. He obviously hadn't shaved in days, and his wrinkled clothes looked as if he'd slept in them. Yet there was enough of a resemblance that it was like looking at himself in the mirror, except for the tortured expression branded deep in his brother's eyes.

"You can't help. You're never here to help."

Bull's-eye. The barb hit deep. Guilt clogged his throat. Jack was right. He did keep leaving, returning to Cedar Bluff because he wanted a normal life. At his brother's expense. "I'm sorry, Jack. I'm here now. I can help you." Jadon kept his tone calm and reassuring. "Everything is going to be fine."

"It's not fine." Jack spun away, his movements jerky and agitated. "It's bad, Jadon. The voices are bad. Telling me to do bad things."

His heart sank. The voices were back. The same voices that had told Jack to set his apartment building on fire four months ago. He couldn't imagine how awful it must be for Jack to be tormented like this. What had happened to the new medication regime that had been working so well?

"You're not a bad person, Jack. You're tired and scared. I'm here to keep you safe. Come with me so we can go back to the hospital and get some help."

"No!" Jack swept his arm across the top of the dresser, sending various picture frames and sports memorabilia crashing to the floor. "You don't understand what it's like. I'm not going back to the hospital."

Once the police arrived his brother would have no choice. It was a pattern that had repeated itself too many times to count. He tried to hang on to his patience, knowing he'd pushed too hard, too fast, because he'd wanted this to be over so he could head back to Cedar Bluff.

To Alyssa and his daughters.

"I thought you liked Dr. Cranberg?" Jadon asked, keeping his tone casual, nonthreatening. "I thought things were going better with her?"

"I do like Dr. Liz. She's nice." For a moment uncertainty shone in Jack's eyes. "She doesn't think I'm crazy."

"You're not crazy, Jack." Man, he hated that term. "Let's go see Dr. Liz. I'll go with you." Jadon kept his voice calm even as he inched closer, knowing he'd take his brother down by force if he had to. One reason he always told his mother to stay out of the way, calling him instead.

Jack clutched his hair with both hands, his face twisting into a mask of anguish. "Make them stop, Jadon," he pleaded in a low, tortured tone. "Make the voices stop."

"I will, Jack." He reached his brother, sighing in relief. He took Jack's arm, giving his brother a sideways hug, knowing the worst of the confrontation was over. "I will. Come with me."

Jack's shoulders drooped and he followed Jadon down the stairs to the main floor of the house. When Jadon saw the police had arrived, he warned them back with a shake of his head, leading Jack to his own car instead.

He'd drive Jack to the hospital. The cops could follow if they wanted to. He wanted to discuss Jack's care with Dr. Cranberg. For now this was the best he could do for his brother.

For himself.

How selfish was he, to want a normal life with Alyssa and their daughters when it was clear Jack would never have anything close to that kind of future?

Bleakly, he watched as Jack muttered to himself, curled in the corner of his passenger seat. Maybe Jack was right. Maybe him leaving to go back to Cedar Bluff wasn't helping.

But what could he do? Move to Madison? He'd considered that option before, but not now. Not with having Alyssa and the girls to consider. Gretchen was doing better the last time he'd called in, but they still needed him.

Yet so did Jack.

Thankfully, this episode had ended without violence. But they hadn't all ended this peacefully. Even so, the situation had been stressful, which was exactly why he still hadn't told Alyssa the truth.

There was a small, selfish part of him that didn't want her to meet Jack. To see what his life with his twin brother was really like. She didn't need any more stress. If he had his way, he'd keep Grace, Gretchen and even Alyssa in a protective cocoon, safe from the harsh realities of life.

Jack moaned and mumbled something under his breath and Jadon prayed his brother would stay calm until they'd been able to see Dr. Liz.

At the hospital, the staff quickly admitted Jack for an inpatient psychiatric stay. The police had followed with his parents, doing the necessary paperwork to keep Jack under strict observation for his own safety.

"The new medication was working," his mother said in a low voice a while later, once they'd finished and were waiting in the lobby. "For a while he was doing better. I don't know what happens to him, why he suddenly stops taking his pills."

He didn't know either. Just more proof that his mother and his brother needed him. "Jack needs to stay in the inpatient program where they regulate his medication closely," he said, drawing in a deep, heavy sigh. "But he has to stay voluntarily, we can't force him. At least this episode wasn't as bad as the last one. Has he been staying away from those useless friends he'd been tangled up with?"

"I don't know for sure, but I think so," his mother said. "He seemed to be doing everything that Dr. Liz asked of him."

Jadon hoped so. His brother had gotten mixed up with a bad crowd, and under their negative influence Jack had become much worse. In fact, his brother had owed some of them a lot of money, which Jadon had figured out after he'd been jumped and robbed the last time he'd come home.

He'd suspected at the time they'd thought he was Jack. Just like when they'd been kids, Jack's troubles had often rubbed off on him. Because people couldn't tell them apart.

He'd suffered more than once for Jack's sins. Yet he couldn't hold his brother responsible for being sick either.

"He'll stay an inpatient now for a while, won't he?" his mother asked, drawing Jadon out of his reverie.

"Yes, he'll be an inpatient for a while." Probably not long enough. Psychiatric programs were losing money and government funding, making the inpatient programs few and far between. And in most cases the patient had to agree to stay.

"Will you stay for a few days and talk to his doctor?" his mother asked. She glanced at his father, and he wondered why there were together. Had his father officially divorced his second wife? Were his parents thinking of getting back together again?

"I can't. I have to get back to Cedar Bluff."

His mother's eyes widened in surprised dismay. "You can't! What if something happens?"

The old familiar guilt made him waver. Should he stay? His mother deserved to have a normal life, too. Heaven knew, she'd given up a lot. Didn't he owe Jack and his mother at least some of his precious time?

Yes, but so did Alyssa. He had other responsibilities now and the two were tearing him apart. He'd wanted to keep them separate but maybe he was deluding himself.

Thinking of Alyssa, Grace and Gretchen waiting for him at the hospital made him shake his head. "I can't. Mom, there's something you need to know. You're a grandmother, grandparents," he amended, including his father in the announcement. "I have twin daughters, Grace Aubrey and Gretchen Louise. They were born just a few days ago."

"Twins?" his mother repeated in stunned surprise. She couldn't have looked more shocked if he'd announced he'd been kidnapped by wild monkeys. "My goodness, you're married?"

"No," he said grimly. Marriage was not an option. Convincing Alyssa to stay with him on a temporary basis was hard enough. And what more could he ask? Jack's difficulties weren't easy to handle. Some families weren't meant to stay together. "The babies were born prematurely and the smaller one, Gretchen, has had some complications. We haven't had time to really think about the future."

"I see." His mother fell silent and he knew she was upset and hurt that he hadn't brought Alyssa over to meet her. Or that he hadn't invited her to Cedar Bluff to meet Alyssa.

How could he explain a relationship he wasn't sure he had?

"Look, a lot has happened. Alyssa is being discharged today from the hospital. I need to get back. I'm sure you'll meet Alyssa soon, maybe at Christmas." His voice lacked conviction, but he couldn't help it. He didn't really want Alyssa to be a part of his problems with Jack.

"All right." His mother looked a bit forlorn, but he noticed his father stepped closer, adding his support. Seeing his parents together again after so many years made him wonder what would be different the second time around. Did his parents have what it took to stick together this time if things went bad with Jack again? Love couldn't solve everything.

"Dad, it was good to see you again." He made an effort to mend the rift of the past, thinking about how he'd feel if his daughters remained angry at him for years on end. Not good. He forced a smile. "I'll be in touch with both of you about our plans for the holiday."

"Bye, Jadon." As he turned to leave, he heard his mother exclaim, "Grandparents! Can you believe we're actually grandparents, Josh?"

"Good news," his father agreed. "And about time."

Jadon felt bad, knowing he should have asked them right then and there to come back with him to meet their grandchildren.

But first he needed some time alone with Alyssa.

* * *

Outside, it had started snowing again. Good thing his parents hadn't come with him to meet Alyssa after all. The roads were slick, forcing him to drive much more slowly than he wanted to. At one point a woman spun out in front of him, hitting the median of the interstate and coming to a jarring stop. He'd gone over to help her, to confirm she wasn't badly hurt, and had waited with her for the police to arrive before going back out on the highway again.

He headed to the hospital first, even though it was late, nearly eight o'clock at night by the time he made it back to Cedar Bluff. He'd called Alyssa's cell phone, but it had gone immediately to voice mail, indicating she didn't have her phone turned on. He pulled into the hospital parking lot and shut off the engine.

The hospital wasn't a white building, like so many of them were, but had been structured with a dark brown cedar wood which made it stand out starkly against the snow-covered trees. In the summer the building meshed with the wooded landscape, but not now. A brightly lit Christmas wreath hung over the front door, a welcoming beacon through the swirling snow.

Inside, the warmth and the muted Christmas music engulfed him. Odd that being in the hospital felt very much like coming home.

Alyssa wasn't in the nursery. He spent a few minutes with Grace and Gretchen, amazed and relieved at how well Gretchen was doing without her mask.

She looked so much better without it.

As much as he wanted to stay and hold his daughters, he really needed to find Alyssa. No doubt Simon had driven her to his house. Braving the snow-covered streets once again, he headed home.

But the house was dark. Not a single light shone through the windows. Frowning, he glanced at the clock. Had she gone to bed already? It was early, but she was no doubt exhausted.

Inside, he flipped on the lights as he walked through the kitchen and into the living room. He expected her to be on the sofa, since he'd taken down her bedroom set, but she wasn't. If she'd made herself at home in his bed, she couldn't be that upset with him. Treading softly, he opened the door to his room.

Empty.

Alyssa wasn't here, waiting for him.

He tried not to become alarmed. If she wasn't at the hospital and she wasn't here, where was she? At her apartment, without a bed? Or staying with Seth and Kylie?

He called her cell phone again without a response. Then he called the hospital to get Seth's number. Kylie answered the phone and confirmed that Alyssa wasn't with them.

"Sorry to bother you," he mumbled, hanging up before Kylie could ask all sorts of questions. Questions he couldn't answer.

Feeling panicky and desperate to find Alyssa, he drove to her apartment building. The snow-covered hill made things tricky, but he managed to get up to the top. He noticed Alyssa's car in her parking space and stared at it for a moment, thinking back.

She'd worked on Wednesday night, and had driven herself to work. Then he'd taken her home to his place, where she'd stayed until she'd gone into labor.

Her car shouldn't have been here, unless Alyssa had found it in the parking garage and had driven herself home.

Relieved to have that mystery solved, he went up to the main door and pressed on her buzzer. When there was no answer, he delved into his pocket, finding the keys she'd given him when he'd moved her things.

Letting himself inside, he took the stairs two at a time to get up to her second-floor apartment. He didn't bother knocking at the door but used the key to get in.

Alyssa was asleep on her sofa. Breathing a sigh of relief, he crossed over to her, reaching down to gently shake her awake.

"Alyssa? I'm back."

"Jadon?" She opened her eyes and blinked at him. "How did you get in?"

"I still had your key. How did you get in?"

She swung up to a sitting position, pushing her hair out of her face. "Mr. Worthington let me in."

He swallowed hard and dropped down beside her. "I'm sorry about this morning. Remember I told you about my family crisis?"

Warily, she nodded. "Yes. You didn't want to go into detail at the time," she said.

"I know. Partly because I didn't want you to worry or to be stressed out." He knew he was botching up the explanation. "Let me start at the beginning. Remember I mentioned I had a brother?"

When she nodded, he braced himself. "Jack is more than just my brother. He's my twin. My identical twin."

CHAPTER THIRTEEN

ALYSSA stared at Jadon, trying to comprehend what he was saying. Half-asleep, she was certain the neurons in her brain weren't working properly.

Because she could have sworn he'd just told her he had a twin brother.

"I know it's a shock, and I'm sorry I didn't tell you sooner," Jadon was saying. "But Jack has a few…emotional problems. Rather serious problems."

A deep coldness washed over her body, seeping down into her bones. She felt slow and somewhat confused, very much like the day she'd slipped and fallen into Lake Michigan. "A twin," she repeated carefully. "With emotional problems."

Jadon's Adam's apple bobbed nervously in his neck. "Yes. I can't lie to you. My parents divorced before Jack and I started high school. The stress of coping with Jack's illness eroded their marriage."

Her mouth went dry as she thought of little Grace and Gretchen. Was Jack's problem hereditary? Was that why he'd kept it a secret? "What illness does he have?" she asked, dreading the answer.

Jadon lifted a hand, his tone pleading. "I know what

you're thinking and there's no reason to suspect that our daughters will also inherit Jack's illness. No one in my family, or in my extended family, has the same problems as Jack. No one."

She wanted to believe him. More than anything, she wanted to believe her daughters would be fine. But he still hadn't answered her question. Her fingers curled into her fists, her nails digging into her palms, although she was oblivious to the pain. "Jadon, what sort of illness does he have?"

"Paranoid schizophrenia." At her stunned expression, he rushed on. "Jack's been getting treatment from a variety of doctors over the years, but this newest doctor, Elizabeth Cranberg, is the area expert in managing this illness. And Jack seemed to like her. But for some reason, like so many other patients with a chronic illness, once he feels better he stops taking his meds. And then he tends to suffer a bad relapse."

Jiminy Cricket, she never would have suspected Jadon's brother had paranoid schizophrenia. She swallowed hard, hearing the exhaustion in his tone. She couldn't even imagine how hard it must be to live with someone with such a debilitating condition.

No wonder Jadon had been so protective of their psych patient Mitch. She understood now why he'd snapped at Susan that night.

He'd lived with someone who was just like Mitch.

"But, Jadon, schizophrenia does tend to run in families," she said, her stomach tied up in knots. She'd learned that much in her psych class. "I'm worried about our daughters."

Jadon's expression was grim. "Normally schizophrenia does run in families. But I researched this extensively the first time I left, and I discovered there are other reasons people come down with a form of schizophrenia. Jack was a wild child when we were young. He got mixed up in a rough crowd during middle school and began experimenting with drugs. That's when we first noticed his behavior had changed. We put him in treatment several times. Even years later, when his drug screens were finally negative, his behavior was still erratic. I got him in to see Dr. Elizabeth Cranberg and she confirmed that his case didn't show the classic signs of schizophrenia. She thought it was more likely related to his drug use, especially as there is no family history."

Had Jadon worried about coming down with the disease, too? Being Jack's identical twin, he must have thought about the possibility. She couldn't imagine how he must have felt, watching his twin and wondering if he might be next.

"Is that why you told me you weren't interested in a long-term relationship when we first met?" she asked.

Jadon momentarily closed his eyes, his expression pained. "Yes. I didn't tell you the truth from the very beginning because I was embarrassed. Maybe a little ashamed. I've had to live with the stigma of mental illness my whole life. My family has struggled for a long time. Jack's illness ruined my parents' marriage and then, when my father remarried, his second wife couldn't cope either. You can see why I'd never planned on making a commitment."

The truth still had the power to hurt. Obviously if she hadn't fallen pregnant, they wouldn't be sitting here, having this conversation.

She felt nauseous. The last thing she'd planned to do was to trap Jadon into something he didn't want. Something he'd gone to great lengths to avoid.

The same way her mother had inadvertently trapped her father. Who'd left once the novelty of being a parent had worn off. She knew comparing Jadon to her father wasn't fair—he at least accepted his responsibilities. But she wanted more.

"I always thought you didn't care about me, as you never once talked about your feelings."

"I do care about you, Alyssa. Very much. I missed you more than I ever would have imagined. But then Jack needed me and I used him as an excuse to leave. I came back, thinking of getting in touch with you, only to find out you were pregnant."

"And me being pregnant meant more responsibility for you," she guessed in a low tone.

"Not just that," he argued. "Alyssa, I'm trying to protect you, to keep you and our daughters away from the stress of dealing with Jack's illness."

After seeing Mitch, she could somewhat understand what he meant. "Are you saying he's violent?"

"Psych patients are unpredictable. They're really not violent very often, unless provoked. Jack and I were in an argument once and a former girlfriend of mine got in the middle of it, making things worse, and he shoved her, knocking her right off her feet." Jadon's lips thinned. "I didn't blame her when she broke off our relationship."

Dear heaven. She could only imagine. Yet she didn't like his fatalistic attitude. "So where does that leave us?"

He slowly shook his head. "I don't know. Jack is my

responsibility, not yours. I don't want the same thing that happened to my parents to happen to us."

She wanted to be glad Jadon had finally opened up about his feelings, admitting he at least cared for her, but her thrill of hope was overshadowed by his news.

Could she really live with the stress he described? On top of having preemie twins? She honestly wasn't sure.

"I stopped by the hospital on my way home," he said. "Gretchen looks so much better with her mask off."

Alyssa nodded, grateful for the change in subject. "Yes, she does. I'm relieved both girls are doing well. If they don't have any more complications, and continue to gain weight, Dr. Downer thought they'd probably come home by Christmas."

"The perfect Christmas present," Jadon said with a smile.

She couldn't smile back, already thinking of how Jadon would want to go home to see his family for Christmas. Without her and their daughters. Deep down, she could admit that while she'd been determined to be happy raising the girls alone, she'd also secretly wanted a traditional two-parent family. But Jadon wasn't free to be a part of her family. Not the way she wanted. The magnitude of their problems seemed greater and greater.

"Alyssa, I know I don't have much to offer you, but I'd still like to take you back to my house."

Earlier, she'd wanted nothing more than to go back with Jadon. Had been upset that he'd left her again. But now she wanted more than their half relationship.

She wanted it all. She wanted love and commitment.

"I'm sorry, Jadon. But I can't. Not right now." Maybe not ever, if he wasn't willing to try.

He stared at her for a long moment. "Alyssa, you don't even have a bed to sleep in. At least come back to my place so you can get some rest."

She shook her head. "I'm fine here, really. And I have my car, too. Please understand, I need time. Time to assimilate what you've told me."

He dropped his head in his hands in apparent defeat. "All right. But please call me. No matter what you need."

"I will."

Jadon slowly stood and moved toward the doorway. He stopped, glanced back at her as if he wanted to say something, but then remained silent as he let himself out of her apartment, gently closing the door behind him.

Alyssa stretched out on the sofa, feeling overwhelmed and exhausted. A twin brother with emotional disturbances. No wonder Jadon rarely talked about his feelings. He'd probably learned early on to repress his emotions when his brother was acting out. She'd fallen in love with him, but Jadon hadn't said anything about love. He was certainly a pro at handling responsibility, though.

She and the babies were just more responsibilities for him to deal with.

Jadon drove back to his house, feeling sick again. His idea of keeping his two families separate had seemed like a good compromise, but the anxious expression in Alyssa's eyes when he'd told her about Jack's problems convinced him he'd been right all along. The stress would be too much.

Deep down, he knew it was better that he'd come clean with the truth.

He cared about her too much to expose her to the same problems his parents had faced.

And as much as he wanted nothing more than to be with Alyssa, to watch Grace and Gretchen as they grew, he couldn't renounce his brother.

Jack was his responsibility, too.

Did he have to give up one family to care for the other?

He pulled into his driveway, trudging up to the cold, empty house.

An impossible situation, no matter which way he looked at it.

Jadon didn't get much sleep. Using his palms to rub the grit from his burning eyes, he staggered to the bathroom, hoping a shower would make a difference in how he felt.

No such luck.

On the way out of the shower, he stopped outside the new nursery, a wave of hopelessness overwhelming him. Would he and Alyssa have to agree to some sort of joint-custody arrangement? He couldn't imagine she'd do that willingly, and how could he push the issue when the twins were still so small?

He turned away from the smiling ballerinas in the pictures hanging over the two cribs, set against pale pink walls he'd painted late into the middle of the night as a surprise for Alyssa. It hurt to remember how excited he'd been, how he'd agonized over the decor, hoping and praying Alyssa would like what he'd done. For her. For their family.

Talk about being in a state of denial. Fantasizing about having a family with Alyssa had been nothing more than an idealistic dream. How could he have forgotten, even for a moment, the impact of Jack's illness?

He turned away from the cheerful nursery to head into the kitchen. His appetite had disappeared so he settled for a cup of coffee, sipping out of his mug and staring sightlessly outside. The snow from last night had stopped, and the warmth of the sun had burned away the clouds, glimmering brightly off the newly fallen snow.

If only the sun could warm his heart, too.

As he was scheduled to work nights, he decided to go to the hospital early to visit the girls, figuring he could try to get some sleep later.

The drive to Cedar Bluff Hospital was short and within fifteen minutes he walked into the nursery, not entirely surprised to see Alyssa had already arrived. The rapt expression on her face was so poignantly serene as she rocked back and forth, nursing Grace, it stopped him in his tracks.

His chest tightened painfully, making it difficult to breathe. She'd never looked so beautiful.

So content.

He loved her. The knowledge hit like a truckload of Christmas trees. Good grief, he loved her. Loved Alyssa with all his heart and soul. Had begun to fall in love with her even before he'd had to leave to rescue Jack all those months ago. The idea that he could be intimate with her and yet keep his heart isolated from her was laughable.

She was everything he'd wanted in a wife, a mother for his children.

And in some dark region of his mind he realized the best thing he could do for her, and for Grace and Gretchen, was to provide for them financially while keeping them far away from the impact of his messed-up family.

Which meant keeping them distant from himself, too.

Alyssa felt Jadon's gaze and glanced up from where Grace was successfully nursing to look at him.

The admiration in his heated glance made her mouth go dry. For a moment they stared at each other, but then he broke the connection, looking away, and the expression was gone.

Had she imagined it? She didn't think so.

She swallowed hard and glanced back down at Grace, confused all over again. She'd pretty much made up her mind to accept losing Jadon and the family she'd always wanted.

But now she wasn't so sure.

"Gracie is nursing better, isn't she?" Jadon asked in a low voice, as if to not disturb the baby.

She nodded. "Gretchen still doesn't nurse very much, but Grace is becoming a pro. She doesn't nurse for long, but as long as she's gaining weight, I'm happy."

"Has she?" Jadon stepped closer. "Gained weight, I mean."

"Yes, two full ounces." She never would have realized just how important the smallest accomplishment was for a preemie. But gaining two ounces was a very big deal.

Gretchen hadn't gained weight—in fact, she'd lost another ounce, probably a result of her time wearing the CPAP mask and battling pneumonia.

Although the mask was off, Alyssa knew Gretchen wasn't completely out of the woods yet. The tiny twin wasn't nearly as strong as Grace.

"Wonderful. And Gretchen?" he asked.

She shook her head. "No, down another ounce."

For a long moment Jadon stared down into Gretchen's isolette. The baby was getting a tube feeding, so they couldn't hold her until the feeding was finished.

"Jack is older than me by about two and a half minutes," Jadon mused. "But he was much larger than I was, almost a full pound. The doctor said that sometimes one twin can actually steal nourishment from the second twin, especially in cases where the twins are identical, sharing one placenta."

"Really?" She hadn't known that. Good thing Grace and Gretchen hadn't been that far apart in weight, although they were also fraternal and not identical twins. "How big were you?"

"Only two and a half pounds," Jadon said. "My mother said I was in the neonatal ICU for a full week longer than Jack. And because I was so small, and needed so much more care, both she and my dad focused all their attention on me."

She began to see where Jadon's bout of reminiscing was going. "Do you think that's why Jack went a little wild when he was older? Because he was always competing for your parents' attention?"

Jadon tucked his hands in his pockets and lifted a shoulder. "I imagine that could be one theory. Despite my small size, and being delayed as a baby, doing all the normal milestones of sitting, crawling, walking and so on, I always did well in school."

"Better than Jack?" she guessed.

He nodded. "Yeah. It wasn't that Jack wasn't smart, but he certainly didn't try as hard."

"So you feel guilty? Like it was your fault your parents paid too much attention to you and not enough to Jack?" she asked, already suspecting the answer.

"Isn't it?" he countered. "Not that I did it on purpose, obviously, but it's something I always wonder about. Let's face it, if I had been the older twin, and Jack the younger, smaller twin, don't you think it's possible our lives would have been different?"

She swallowed hard, hating to admit he might have a point. No wonder he'd been so adamant that she pay attention to Grace, too, during Gretchen's illness. Even now, despite his reassurances otherwise, he was worried that history might repeat itself with Grace and Gretchen.

Glancing down at Grace, who'd fallen asleep, Alyssa traced the tip of her index finger over her daughter's dainty features, and vowed not to let that happen.

"At least now that we know, we won't make the same mistake as parents," she said slowly.

Jadon didn't answer as she stood and placed the sleeping Grace back into her isolette.

"I know you said you needed time," Jadon said in a low voice. "But I want you to know the offer of staying with me, at least for a while, is still open. I'm concerned about your ability to manage caring for the twins without help."

Alyssa wavered. He was being the responsible one

again. Jadon had opened up about himself, more than he ever had. Which offered some hope. Yet she knew, once she took that step of going home with him, it would be very hard to go back.

Should she fight for her love? Or would that be a constant uphill battle? And was she strong enough to handle the impact of Jack's illness on top of caring for Grace and Gretchen?

"At least think about it," Jadon advised. "I'm working night shift tonight and tomorrow night, so it's not as if I'll be there much."

Reassuring her he wouldn't be there much didn't sound promising. Were they back to being parents in name only? Ironic that she'd already come to feel as if his house was a home.

Their home.

She missed Jadon. And she missed her lopsided Charlie Brown Christmas tree. She needed to take a chance, to see if she could somehow bridge the gap between them.

"All right," she agreed. "But only as a trial to see how well I can manage with the girls."

CHAPTER FOURTEEN

ALYSSA second-guessed her decision several times over as she followed Jadon's car through the streets to his house.

Yet when she entered the living room, surprised to find a variety of brand-new Christmas decorations, including a wreath over the fireplace, a nativity scene and tiny twinkling lights strung around the living-room windows, she realized how wonderful it felt to be there with him.

"Here, I'll take your coat," Jadon said, treating her as a guest rather than someone who might be living there. She hid a pang of disappointment.

"Thanks." She crossed over to her lopsided Charlie Brown Christmas tree and gave the drooping branches a welcoming pat. "I see you didn't toss him out for a bigger, better tree," she observed. "And you've been giving him water."

"Of course I've been giving him water. The needles are already starting to fall off. They don't need another excuse."

She smiled, knowing he was right. The poor tree would be lucky to last until the holiday.

"So why didn't you replace him, then?"

"Because this tree obviously held a special place in your heart, and that was more important than how the room looked."

A warm feeling filled her chest. Jadon did care. And if he cared, maybe he could learn to love. He certainly understood her better than she'd thought.

"I...uh, put all the baby stuff into the bedroom," Jadon said, coming up to stand beside her.

Surprised, she glanced up at him. "You did?"

He nodded and she brushed past him, filling her senses with his musky scent as she went over to investigate. In the doorway of the spare bedroom she stopped and stared, realizing he'd done far more than simply set up the baby things.

He'd fully decorated the entire nursery.

"Oh, my," she whispered, her heart melting at the obvious care and concern Jadon had put into every detail. Not only did he have the two cribs set up, and the dressers with changing tables across their tops strategically placed near each one, but he'd painted the walls a soft pink, had hung a border of tiny pink and white ballerina slippers around the entire room, and displayed two portraits of ballerinas on the walls above each crib. In one corner of the room he'd set a gleaming wooden rocker with comfy pink cushions, the perfect spot to rock and nurse the babies.

Completely overwhelmed, she didn't know what to say. The Christmas decorations were special, but this additional surprise was beyond words. Maybe he didn't talk about his feelings much, but his actions had definitely shown them. "Jadon, this is absolutely beautiful."

His smile didn't quite reach his eyes. "I hoped you'd

like it. And don't worry about the sleeping arrangements. I'd planned on putting a sleeper sofa into my office anyway, so I can sleep on the living-room sofa until it's delivered. In the meantime, you can have the bedroom."

Sleeping arrangements? She glanced at him, but he avoided direct eye contact, confirming her suspicions. He'd obviously planned on the two of them sharing the master bedroom.

Because he cared about her? Or was starting to love her?

Swallowing hard, she simply nodded, knowing she still wanted to share a bedroom with him, badly.

"So this is what you were working on while I was in the hospital," she guessed, changing the subject to something safer. No wonder he'd looked so awful those few days, as if he hadn't had any sleep. By the extent of the completed nursery, he couldn't have slept much if at all. "Not just the Christmas decorations, but the nursery, too."

"Yeah. I wanted it all to be a surprise." He looked uncomfortable for a few moments, then said, "I'm going to take a short nap as I'm working tonight."

"Of course. Use the bedroom. Don't argue," she interjected, as he opened his mouth to do just that. "It's going to be difficult enough for you to sleep in the middle of the day, especially with how sunny it is, without trying to do that in the middle of the living room."

He hesitated, but then acquiesced, murmuring, "Thanks," as he headed into the bedroom, gently closing the door behind him.

Alyssa felt curiously lonely without Jadon's presence. In fact, suddenly she felt very much like the guest and not someone who belonged here. She tried to rest for a bit in the living room, thrilled at the festive atmosphere, but then found herself going back into the nursery and picking up one of the matching pink elephants as she settled into the rocking chair. It was all too easy to imagine how cozy things would be once the girls came home.

But this arrangement was only temporary, wasn't it?

They couldn't just simply share parenting duties and nothing else. A family in name only? No, it would never work.

She loved him too much.

And she wanted a happy family. And Jadon's love, forever. She wanted it all.

For the first time in months, since the day she'd discovered she was pregnant and had been unable to get in touch with Jadon, she allowed tears to slip down her cheeks.

Her heart and soul ached for what she'd never have.

Jadon couldn't sleep. Sleeping in the middle of the day had never been easy for him but, with everything seemingly falling apart around him, rest was more elusive than ever.

He stared at the ceiling over his bed, trying not to relive the moment when Alyssa had seen the nursery, her eyes lighting up with excitement and pleasure.

He'd once hoped she'd feel as if she belonged here. With him. With the girls, too.

Marriage was such a huge step. One he hadn't planned on taking. Alyssa deserved marriage, full commitment. Because they'd made a family with Grace and Gretchen.

Yet Jack was family, too. His brother.

His cell phone rang, startling him badly, making him swear under his breath at how he'd forgotten to silence the ringer as he fumbled in his discarded clothes for the instrument.

His stomach twisted when he realized the caller was his mother. "Mom? What's wrong? Jack can't possibly be out of the hospital already?"

"No, nothing is wrong," she quickly assured him. "Ah, actually, we're here to see you."

"Here? In Cedar Bluff?" Jadon shot out of bed, frantically searching for his pants, imagining his parents were right now standing outside his front door.

"Yes, we're at a restaurant on Main Street. What's it called, Josh?" she asked his father. "Oh, yes, The Spinnaker. The food was excellent."

He tugged on his pants, cradling the phone between his shoulder and his ear, hardly able to believe his parents had shown up in Cedar Bluff. "Ah, okay. That's not far away."

"We were hoping we could come to your house and then visit the babies, Grace and Gretchen."

Momentarily closing his eyes, he let out a soundless sigh. Of course they wanted to visit the babies. He couldn't blame them. But he needed to talk to Alyssa about this, too. So much for keeping his two families separate. "Why don't you come here first to meet Alyssa?"

"That would be nice," his mother agreed, sounding excited.

He gave her directions that she repeated for his father. He hung up and sank down onto the edge of his bed, running his fingers nervously through his hair. He was nervous. What would Alyssa think?

His parents hadn't brought Jack, but what if Jack discovered the news about the twins? He'd want to see them, too.

There was no use dwelling on all the complications. He had to deal with his parents first.

He pulled himself together and finished getting dressed. He opened his bedroom door and hesitated, seeing the nursery door was still ajar, and went with his instincts to search for Alyssa in there.

He saw her sitting in the rocking chair, clutching one of the pink elephants to her chest, tears glistening in streaks down her cheeks.

"Alyssa? What's wrong?" Alarmed, he crossed the room to kneel beside her.

"Nothing. Everything." She swiped at her eyes, offering a pathetic attempt at a smile.

He couldn't stand it. Rising to his feet, he took her hand and drew her up and into his arms. "Shh, it's okay. Everything is going to be fine."

She buried her face against his chest, shaking her head as if she disagreed with him.

"Yes, it will. I promise." He kissed the top of her head, smoothing a hand down her back, offering comfort in the only way he knew how. He wasn't sure how he'd fix it, but he wanted to find a way. For her.

Slowly the tension eased out of her body and she melted against him in a way that caused his own body to harden in awareness. Knowing that intimacy was impossible for more reasons than just one, he forced himself to ignore the discomfort.

The doorbell pealed. Alyssa lifted her head from his chest.

"Someone's here," she said, rubbing her face as if to erase the evidence of her tears.

"My parents."

"Your parents?" Her gaze widened in shock.

"I'll get rid of them if you want me to."

Just that quickly, the shocked surprise turned into exasperation. She swiped the dampness from her face. "They're your parents. You can't just get rid of them. Not when they've come all this way to see you."

Still unsure, he nodded. Maybe one, slightly dysfunctional family was better than trying to divide his time between two families? There was only one way to find out. He held out his hand. "Come on, I'd like to introduce you."

She trustingly placed her hand in his. "I thought they were divorced?" she asked as they walked into the living room.

"They are, but I think maybe they're working on getting back together." Jadon still was a little surprised by that revelation himself. The absence of a wedding ring on his dad's hand and the way he seemed to be renewing a relationship with his mother had convinced him his dad had ditched his second wife. Or, more likely, she'd ditched him.

He opened the front door to find his parents anxiously waiting on the front porch. "Come on in, Mom. Dad."

His parents entered the house, their gazes immediately seeking Alyssa, who stood near the center of the living room.

"Alyssa, these are my parents, Janet and Josh Reichert," he said, performing the introductions. "Mom, Dad, this is Alyssa Knight."

Alyssa's tremulous smile betrayed her nerves. "It's nice to meet you," she said.

"It's so nice to meet you, too." His mother wasn't shy, but crossed right over to envelop Alyssa in an enthusiastic hug. "We're so glad you and Jadon found each other. And we just can't wait to see the babies. Twin girls."

Alyssa's smile faltered a little as she glanced over at Jadon, her brow raised questioningly. He tried to reassure her with his gaze that the decision was hers.

He'd abide by her wishes.

Alyssa found herself immediately warming to Jadon's parents. They were both so nice and friendly it was difficult not to like them.

And as they chatted, she began to hope that the fact Jadon had told his parents about the girls meant he was planning a future together.

"Of course you're welcome to see the babies," she told them.

They all climbed into Jadon's car, talking as he negotiated the short distance to Cedar Bluff Hospital, the brown building standing out starkly against the white snow. She told his parents about the labor and delivery, having to go back and repeat the entire story about how she'd fallen into Lake Michigan, which had sent her into early labor. They were horrified and thankful everyone was all right.

Inside the hospital, Jadon's parents commented

about how friendly the staff were when they were constantly greeted by people she and Jadon knew.

"That's why I like it here so much," Jadon explained to his parents. "It's like everyone is part of a family."

Up in the nursery, Jadon's mother started crying when she saw the babies. Jadon's dad held her with a sturdy arm around her shoulders and Alyssa's, though his own eyes seemed a bit moist as he gazed down at the two isolettes holding Grace and Gretchen.

"They're just beautiful," Janet said, reaching over to give Alyssa another hug as she sniffled loudly. "My granddaughters."

"Would you both like to hold them?" she offered, feeling very much like a proper daughter-in-law.

When they both nodded, she fetched warm blankets and wrapped Grace and then Gretchen, handing one baby to each of Jadon's parents. They settled into the two rockers, rapt expressions of sheer wonder on their faces.

"Thank you," Jadon murmured as they stood back, allowing his parents some time with the babies.

"For what?"

"Allowing them to visit."

"Did you think I wouldn't?"

He shrugged. "I wasn't sure."

She stared at him, realizing he would truly have stood by whatever decision she'd made. If she'd thought the situation would bring too much stress, he would have turned them away. Love shone from his eyes and she realized that with Jadon actions spoke much louder than words.

He'd shown her how much he cared in everything he'd done for her. Why had she been so hung up on the words?

He was offering her the family she'd always wanted.

Maybe it wasn't perfect, she knew there would be challenges to face with Jadon's twin brother, Jack, but did she really have anything to complain about? No family was completely perfect, and wasn't it their flaws, along with all the love and laughter, that made the whole package?

And worrying about illnesses of any kind, emotional disturbances, cancer, pick-the-disease-of-your-choice was ridiculous. There was no predicting the future. There was no point to living your life in fear.

"Jadon, I would never keep you or your family away from the girls. Ever."

"Really?" He didn't look sure.

"Yes. And I hope someday you'll allow us to be a part of your family, too."

Instead of closing down his emotions, a glimpse of hopeful surprise gleamed in his eyes. And she understood he didn't want to be the cause of distress, so she needed to convince him that when you loved someone, you made sacrifices for them.

Wasn't that what Jadon had done with Jack? He'd made many sacrifices, she was sure.

None of this was Jadon's fault. He'd done the best he could, considering the difficult circumstances.

"Alyssa, your girls are the most beautiful babies in the entire nursery," his mother gushed. "Don't you think so, Josh?"

"Absolutely," Jadon's father agreed.

"Thank you. Jadon and I feel the same way."

"Yeah, and we're thrilled they're doing so well," Jadon added, taking her hand in his.

His parents stayed a few more minutes, then stood to leave.

"Do you want to ride home with us?" Jadon asked.

"I think I should stay here, to see if they'll nurse a bit," she told him.

He nodded. "Okay, I'll take my parents back in my car and then come back to pick you up."

She watched them leave, and then turned to try nursing Gretchen, who'd woken up and started crying.

The baby actually latched on for a few minutes and Alyssa was thrilled with the small progress. She then nursed Grace, finishing just as Jadon returned.

"I don't think I've ever seen my parents so excited," he said, grinning broadly. "I think they've always secretly wanted a daughter."

She'd felt like a daughter with them, when she hadn't for a very long time. And it was time to put her fears to rest, fighting for what she wanted. "Jadon, there's something you need to know."

Instantly his smile faded and his gaze turned wary. "What is it?"

Gathering her courage, she blurted, "I love you."

He stared at her, his gaze reserved. "Alyssa, I know you think you love me, but Jack's illness isn't going to magically disappear. I don't think you understand the impact it may have on us. I'll always have to help when he's in trouble."

"Do you think I don't know that?" His comments hurt. "I love you, Jadon, because of who you are. The man who loves his family. The man who supports the people he loves. The man who will be the perfect father for our daughters."

He took a deep breath and let it out slowly. "I love you, too, Alyssa. But I'm afraid. I'm worried our love won't be strong enough to weather the stress of Jack's illness."

"Jadon, everything we've gone through has been easier when we've been together. We'll make it through the tough times. I believe in you and I believe in us. Our love is strong enough to get through anything."

He didn't answer but drew her into his arms for a deep kiss and she could tell he was showing her the best way he could, with actions and words. "I have to be there for Jack, but I promise to love and support you and the girls, too."

"I know." She believed him. And knowing he was committed to helping his brother only made her love him more. He wasn't anything like her father, who hadn't stood by anyone. Jadon was committed to his family. Their family was solid and would support Jack. She was optimistic that if Jack stayed on his medication, he'd be fine. "I think Jack will get better. And if there's anything I can do to help, I will."

Jadon's gaze was full of admiration. "What did I do to deserve you?" he asked.

She smiled, circling his waist with her arms and resting her head on his strong, broad chest. "We deserve each other. I love you, Jadon. With my whole heart. With love, we can do anything."

"I want to believe that, Alyssa. Very much."

His hesitancy didn't bother her. She had enough faith for both of them. She was confident the power of their love would make it work.

No matter what.

EPILOGUE

JADON gazed nervously down at the tiny babies, their faces barely visible through the blankets tucked securely around them in their respective infant car seats.

This was it. Grace and Gretchen were coming home. They wore tiny infant apnea monitors, but otherwise they were just fine. The realization that the two were solely dependent on him and Alyssa made him feel just a little panicky.

Alyssa's eyes were full of excitement. "It's Christmas Eve. It's a miracle that we're able to bring the babies home in time for Christmas."

He swallowed hard and nodded. He thought it was a miracle that they were going to have a family dinner this evening at his house. His mother had already prepared most of the meal so that everything would be ready to go when they arrived.

"Thanks for everything," he said to Louis Downer and Carla, the nurse they'd grown close to over the past two weeks. "Are you ready?" he asked Alyssa, grabbing Grace's car seat.

"Yes." Alyssa gave Louis and Carla quick hugs before picking up Gretchen's infant seat. "I'm ready."

Getting both car seats tucked into the backseat of the car wasn't an easy task, but soon they were on their way home.

"Are you sure about this?" Jadon asked, darting a glance over at Alyssa.

She simply smiled, looking far more relaxed than he was. "Yes, Jadon. I'm sure."

He couldn't seem to mask his own anxiety, but nodded anyway. When he pulled into his driveway, he saw that another car stood in the driveway, behind his mother's.

They were here.

He helped unbuckle the infant seats, which was much easier than getting them strapped in. He handed one of the babies to Alyssa and he took the other.

Inside the house, the scent of honey-roasted ham and cranberries filled the air. His father and his brother were busy setting gaily wrapped gifts beneath Alyssa's lopsided Christmas tree. By pouring gallons of water into the bowl at the base, they'd managed to nurture it along until Christmas. It seemed to fit right in with the rest of his family.

Alyssa's eyes widened when she saw his brother. Jack rose to his feet uncertainly, tucking his hands in the front pockets of his black slacks and gazing wistfully at the infant carrier seats.

His brother had cleaned up nicely, making his resemblance to himself all the more startling. Jack's most recent stay at the hospital had brought some great progress and it had actually been Alyssa's idea to have the entire family together for Christmas. He'd only agreed after discussing the possibility with Dr. Liz, who'd ensured Jack's medication blood levels were within therapeutic range to avoid any erratic episodes before giving her permission for the visit.

"Hi, Jack," Alyssa greeted his brother warmly. "It's great to meet you."

"It's good to meet you, too, Alyssa. Thanks for inviting me to dinner." Jack's earnest expression made Jadon relax a bit. Things were going to be fine.

Alyssa smiled and unbuttoned her coat. "Would you like to meet your nieces?"

"Sure."

Jadon set Grace's infant seat on the couch and took Alyssa's coat from her hands. She unbundled the babies just enough for Jack to see their peacefully sleeping faces.

"This one is Grace Aubrey. She was three pounds, nine ounces at birth. And this one is Gretchen Louise, who was three pounds, three ounces when she was born."

Jack stared at the baby girls in awe. "They're beautiful. Jadon is a very lucky guy."

"Well, I think I'm pretty lucky, too," Alyssa said with a tiny laugh, putting him at ease. Jadon noticed his mother and father exchanged a grateful look.

"Mom, do you need any help in the kitchen?" he asked.

"Nope, I have everything under control," she claimed before disappearing back into her haven.

His father had picked up Jack at the hospital to bring him to Cedar Bluff. Jack would only stay for a short while and then his father would take him back to the hospital.

"Would you like to hold one of the babies?" Alyssa was asking Jack now.

His brother's eyes lit up. "Yes, please."

"Take a seat on the chair over there. You can hold Grace." Alyssa gently drew the baby out of her car seat and carried her over to Jack, who took the precious bundle in his arms as if he were holding the most priceless piece of crystal in the world.

Jadon had to swallow hard and look away. Alyssa was doing everything right. She'd made his brother feel at ease and had trusted him with her most prized possession.

It was perfect, having his entire family together at last.

Later, after dinner was over and everyone had opened their gifts, which included lots of baby clothes for Grace and Gretch, it was time for his brother to leave.

Jadon walked with Jack and his father outside. His father slid inside the car to warm it up, leaving the brothers alone for a minute.

"You have a great family, Jadon," Jack said in a low voice.

"*We* have a great family, Jack," he corrected. "Remember, we're all in this together."

"I finally accepted what Dr. Liz has been telling me about taking my medication for the rest of my life," Jack said slowly. "I realize that if I stop, bad things happen."

Jadon nodded. "I'm glad you're following Dr. Liz's advice. She really cares about you, Jack. We all do."

A ghost of a smile flitted on Jack's mouth. "Yeah, I know. Maybe if I keep taking my medication, I'll have a chance at a normal life someday, too."

Jadon hoped so. He really hoped so. And maybe he and Alyssa together could help Jack better than he'd been able to do alone. Small, delicate snowflakes started to fall, and he threw an arm around Jack's shoulders, giving him a quick embrace. "Take care, Jack. We'll see you at the girls' baptisms in a few weeks."

"I'll look forward to it." Jack returned his embrace, before climbing into the passenger seat beside his father.

Jadon stood, watching them leave, barely feeling the cold snow-kisses as he stared at the spot where his dad's taillights had vanished in the dark night.

Alyssa came outside, shivering. "Hey, it's snowing! Jadon? Are you all right?"

"I'm fine." He turned and hugged her, knowing how lucky he was to have such a wonderful woman in his life. She'd given him such a precious family. "Let's go back inside."

"All right," she agreed.

He waited for her to take a seat near the Christmas tree before kneeling beside her. "I have a Christmas gift for you."

She gasped when she saw the black velvet box. "Jadon?"

"Alyssa, I love you so much. You've made me realize how much stronger we are when we're together. Will you please marry me?" He flipped open the ring box, displaying a dazzling pink diamond engagement ring with a matching wedding band.

Pink. Of course he'd bought her something pink. First, they'd brought the babies home, then they'd had a wonderful family dinner with Jadon's brother. And now a proposal.

Three Christmas miracles in one day. She smiled through happy tears. "Yes, Jadon, I'd be honored to marry you."

"Merry Christmas, Alyssa."

She smiled and kissed him, hugging him tight and vowing to never let go. "Merry Christmas, Jadon."

No Christmas had ever been as special as this.

1109/03a

MEDICAL™ 2-in-1

Coming next month
SNOWBOUND: MIRACLE MARRIAGE
by Sarah Morgan

Confirmed bachelor Dr Daniel Buchannan is babysitting his brother's children and needs help! Nurse Stella, his ex-fiancée, reluctantly rescues him and, snowbound with his makeshift family, Daniel realises he can never let Stella go again…

CHRISTMAS EVE: DOORSTEP DELIVERY
by Sarah Morgan

After an unforgettable night with bubbly midwife Hayley Hamilton, single father Dr Patrick Buchannan finds himself missing a woman he barely knew. But a knock at his door on Christmas Eve is about to change all that!

HOT-SHOT DOC, CHRISTMAS BRIDE
by Joanna Neil

For Dr Josh Bentley, the holiday season equals heartache. But bubbly new colleague Dr Alison Randall believes in white Christmases and all the excitement that goes with them! Can she work the ultimate Christmas miracle and melt this doctor's heart?

CHRISTMAS AT RIVERCUT MANOR
by Gill Sanderson

To newcomers Dr Mike Curtis and his young daughter, it's warm-hearted nurse Grace who really makes Rivercut feel like home. To make this a Christmas Grace will always remember, Mike will bring her back to the manor house…as his bride!

On sale 4th December 2009
Available at WHSmith, Tesco, ASDA, Eason and all good bookshops.
For full Mills & Boon range including eBooks visit
www.millsandboon.co.uk

 # MEDICAL™

Single titles coming next month

FALLING FOR THE PLAYBOY MILLIONAIRE
by Kate Hardy

James Alexander, Penhally Bay's hot-shot new doc,
thought he'd outgrown his playboy reputation, but beautiful
registrar Charlotte Walker is unconvinced! She'll fight her
attraction to James every step of the way, unless James
can persuade Charlotte to put her past behind her
and trust him with her heart!

THE SURGEON'S NEW-YEAR WEDDING WISH
by Laura Iding

Trauma surgeon Leila Ross's new colleague,
Dr Quinn Torres, is the most arrogant man she's ever met
– but undoubtedly the sexiest! Even though she knows
this single dad has closed his heart to love, whenever
he holds Leila in his arms, she secretly longs
for marriage and a family...

On sale 4th December 2009

Available at WHSmith, Tesco, ASDA, Eason and all good bookshops.
For full Mills & Boon range including eBooks visit
www.millsandboon.co.uk

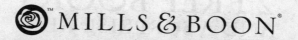

2 FREE BOOKS
AND A SURPRISE GIFT

We would like to take this opportunity to thank you for reading this Mills & Boon® book by offering you the chance to take TWO more specially selected books from the Medical™ series absolutely FREE! We're also making this offer to introduce you to the benefits of the Mills & Boon® Book Club™—

- **FREE home delivery**
- **FREE gifts and competitions**
- **FREE monthly Newsletter**
- **Exclusive Mills & Boon Book Club offers**
- **Books available before they're in the shops**

Accepting these FREE books and gift places you under no obligation to buy, you may cancel at any time, even after receiving your free books. Simply complete your details below and return the entire page to the address below. You don't even need a stamp!

YES Please send me 2 free Medical books and a surprise gift. I understand that unless you hear from me, I will receive 5 superb new stories every month including two 2-in-1 books priced at £4.99 each and a single book priced at £3.19, postage and packing free. I am under no obligation to purchase any books and may cancel my subscription at any time. The free books and gift will be mine to keep in any case.

Ms/Mrs/Miss/Mr _____ Initials _____

Surname _____

Address _____

_____

_____ Postcode _____

Send this whole page to: Mills & Boon Book Club, Free Book Offer, FREEPOST NAT 10298, Richmond, TW9 1BR